PRAISE FOR *HOUSE ARREST* BY MARY MORRIS

"In *House Arrest* Morris weaves a taut story that will haunt readers."
—Anne Morris, *Fort Worth Star-Telegram*

"[Morris's] writing is filled with a sense of how relationships are perpetually mismatched, of how the still zone of indecision is somehow at the heart of life, and how travel can be at once numbing and revelatory."
—James Saynor, *The New York Times Book Review*

"Morris is extremely good at evoking exotic claustrophobia."
—*The New Yorker*

"Morris's simple heartfelt writing allows the reader to see through Conover's eyes, to smell the spiciness of the Caribbean food, to hear the waves crashing against the shore."
—Elizabeth Moore, *Newark Star-Ledger*

"What lifts this book far above its thriller-genre plot outlines are its thematic depth and urgent tone. . . . We can't help but feel a fierce frustration bubbling up in Morris's voice, speaking of confinement, oppression, and clipped wings. . . ."
—Andy Solomon, *St. Petersburg Times*

"Maggie's hopes and fears, as well as those of Isabel, estranged daughter of the island's revolutionary leader, are intimately revealed, allowing us to feel the isolation and desperation that both women experience." —*Library Journal*

"The parallels between *la isla* and Cuba are clear, and the accomplished Mary Morris's ability to create a subdued sense of menace adds a great deal to the generally discomfiting tone of her new novel." —Marilyn Murray Willison, *Miami Herald*

BY MARY MORRIS

Vanishing Animals and Other Stories

Crossroads

The Bus of Dreams

Nothing to Declare:
Memoirs of a Woman Traveling Alone

The Waiting Room

Wall to Wall: From Beijing to Berlin by Rail

The Lifeguard

The Night Sky (previously published as
A Mother's Love)

House Arrest

MARY MORRIS

House Arrest

Picador USA
New York

Picador is a U.S. registered trademark and is used by St. Martin's Press under license from Pan Books Limited.

Although this book contains material from the world in which we live, the characters, the places, and the events are all fiction. All dialogue is invented. Isabel, her family, the inhabitants, and even *la isla* itself are creations of the author's imagination.

Library of Congress Cataloging-in-Publication Data

Morris, Mary.
    House arrest : a novel / Mary Morris.
      p.   cm.
    ISBN 0-312-15547-6
    1. Detention of persons—Caribbean Area—Fiction.
    2. Women—Caribbean Area—Fiction.   3. Caribbean
Area—Fiction. I. Title.
    [PS3563.O87445H68   1997]
    813'.54—dc21   97-800
                                              CIP

First published in the United States of America by
Nan A. Talese, an imprint of Doubleday, a division of
Bantam Doubleday Dell Publishing Group, Inc.

First Picador USA Edition: June 1997

10 9 8 7 6 5 4 3 2 1

This book is for Cristina Garcia, Mark Rudman, and Dani Shapiro, friends who told me it was there and who showed me the way. And to the memory of Jerome Badanes, mentor and friend.

With special thanks to Amanda Urban and Nan A. Talese for all their efforts and support, to Sloan Harris, Jesse Cohen, Diane Marcus, Sol H. Morris for his insightful comments, and, of course, as always, to Larry and Kate for everything.

"For what gives value to travel is fear. It breaks down a kind of inner structure we have. One can no longer cheat—hide behind the hours spent at the office or at the plants (those hours we protest so loudly) which protect us so well from the pain of being alone."

—ALBERT CAMUS

"Will you only let me go? You see, sir . . . traveling is a hard life, but I couldn't live without it."

—FRANZ KAFKA, *The Metamorphosis*

House Arrest

One

THERE ARE NO BIRDS on *la isla*. Isabel told me the first time I came here. If you walk down a country road, there is no flutter of wings, no morning chirps. Deep in the forests and in the swamps, you can still find the trogon, the emerald hummingbird, the pygmy owl, but not near the towns. This is because the people have eaten them all. In the cities there are no pigeons picking at crumbs because there are no crumbs.

There used to be all kinds of birds in the Zoológico Antiguo—rare blue macaws, ruby-throated finches, giant-crested cockatoos. But the looters ate them. They ate the giraffe as well. It is not difficult to see that the people are starving. They have eaten their cats. Their horses too. But they draw the line at dogs. They think that if they eat their dogs, they will eat their children next.

Sometimes they put the dogs to sleep, but mostly they just let them go. Of course, the dogs don't want to go so the people get on buses and ride with them out of town where they hurl them from the windows. On the outskirts of the city, you can see dogs chasing after buses for miles. This is what this country has become, Isabel said, a pack of desperate, starving dogs.

I saw them myself the last time I was here—mutts mostly, but some still with their collars on. They run in feral packs, digging in garbage where almost nothing is thrown out. Everywhere you see the dogs. They roam, scrawny, tails between their legs, through Ciudad del Caballo, the City of the Horse.

Once this ancient city of viceroys and buccaneers, of cobblestone streets and stone citadels, was called Puerto Angélico, named by the Spanish five hundred years ago because of the way the harbor shaped itself into an angel's wings. But with the victory three decades ago they renamed it for the leader whom they have long called the Horse.

Isabel joked with me that he is the only horse left. He is proud, fast, strong, but with blinders on. She told me that he would run back to his burning barn. In the end, she said, horses are not that smart.

Of course it is Isabel I think of as I sit in this room. Not that I have stopped thinking about her for these past two years. I think of her as the shadow that cast itself over my life. I have asked myself many times how it is possible that someone I knew so briefly could have come to occupy so much space. Yet she has assumed the weight of memory. I can still see her clearly. Her bone-thin body, her breasts, the small craters they left in the sand.

My name is Maggie Conover and I am thirty-six years old. I have lived a fairly ordinary life—a childhood in upstate New York, the same marriage and job for the last ten years. Yet for reasons that I cannot understand I have found myself at times in circumstances that others would consider to be extraordinary. This is one of those times. I am writing this down now because I do not know if my story will otherwise be told. I do not know if anyone will know where I have been or what has become of me.

Except for the plastic chairs, the room where they have asked me to wait is small, empty, and white. A wall of blue doors stretches ahead of me, and beyond these doors the officials sit, though most have gone home now. They must know it is cold in this lounge where the air conditioner blasts above my head. It is loud and makes a rattling sound as if a screw is loose inside as it spews cold air on me. If Todd were here, he'd probably try to fix it. He'd tap its side, at least figure out what was wrong. I wish I knew how to do things with my hands. All I can do now is run them up and down my sides while I try to get warm.

The customs officials—both men and women—wear olive green. Olive green combat uniforms, camouflage shirts, stretch pants. Though there's no war, it's all standard-issue military gear. Only a few of the guards stand by with guns but one ambles back and forth, carrying his machine gun like a lunch box. Occasionally they glance my way. When they whisper, I try to imagine what they are saying. Do they think I am pathetic, like a child being punished in the hall? Do they think I am a spy? Do they want to buy my khaki pants?

Just a few hours ago I stepped on the tarmac, into the sultry night. The air was warm and smelled of citrus and the sea. The line in which I stood moved swiftly and the tourists with their jackets and sweaters draped across their arms were all excited, ready to have a good time. Soon I was smiling at the young immigration officer with the dark hair and he smiled back.

Then he glanced at my passport, fondling it as if he'd never seen one before. He studied its number, flipping through the pages of stamps. He stared at my picture, then back at me as if he could not quite match the photo with my face. Perhaps I don't look the way I did when it was taken. Perhaps I looked better then.

The young man seemed to hesitate, unsure of what to do. Behind me a man put down his carry-on, a woman sighed. There was a shuffling of feet as the line of travelers pressed against my back. Then the young immigration officer picked up the phone. *"Un momentito,"* he told me. He spoke softly with his lips close to the receiver, as if he were arranging to meet someone in a secret place. Then, looking up at me, his brown eyes tinged with regret, he asked me to step aside.

So I did. I stepped aside as flights came through from Brussels and Berlin, from Cancún and Moscow. I waited as elegant tourists and shabby tourists and tourists in safari clothes with video cameras breezed through customs. A few times I tried to ask for an explanation, but the immigration officer told me to be patient because he was awaiting a phone call. A formality, he assured me, though already I suspected something wasn't right. *"Un ratito,"* he said, shaping his fingers into the equivalent of an inch.

At first I was not the only one waiting. A man with a beard played video games on his laptop. I glimpsed at his screen as a gobbling creature chased a mouse around. He had a visa problem too. So did the older gentleman in the gray fedora. A married couple with a wailing baby had been waiting for hours. But soon they let the others go.

The man with the laptop gave me a little salute as he left.

"They never get it right," he said. He was an amiable enough person, a gringo who lives on *la isla*. He works in import-export, but he didn't say of what. The husband of the couple with a small child in tears paced, and I could tell his case was cause for some concern. For hours their relatives stood on the other side of the partition, faces pressed to the glass, waving, pleading.

At last, with one sweep of the hand, they were allowed to pass to the other side, where they fell into the arms of weeping grandparents, patient friends. The older man with the fedora sat with a resigned look on his face, but eventually he too was let through. A late flight from Jamaica arrived and the tourists, some wearing dreadlocks and carrying musical instruments, were quickly processed. Then the doors of the airport were locked and I was left alone in the cold room.

Next they took things from me. My camera, my tape recorder, my ticket home. They already had my passport. For hours now I have watched officials, shuffling papers, moving about. Rubbing my arms, I try to determine what had gotten me into this predicament. At first I assumed it had something to do with the update I did the last time I was here.

It is true that I traveled on a tourist's visa, but then I always do. I wrote a soft piece by anyone's standards, describing buildings in disrepair, rubble on the boardwalk. I poked fun at the show at the Club Tropical—the women in their trailing boas and tutus whose sequins flew off as men in toreador pants twirled them. I mentioned prison terms for those who insult the regime, but I spoke of no dissidents, revealed no state secrets.

Recalling all of this, it occurs to me that I am not sitting in this room because of the guidebook I wrote. I am here because of Isabel. I suppose the mistake I made was listening to

Manuel and letting him offer to have me meet her in the first place. I should not have listened to Manuel and I should not have made contact with Isabel, though our first meeting was (or so I still want to believe) coincidental. And then once I made contact—once I understood who she was and what she wanted—I should have stayed away.

Probably I should not have come back at all. Lydia, my sister, told me not to come. Astrologically, the signs were inauspicious from the start. She warned me that the alignment of the stars on the day of my departure was the same as it had been the night of the Playa Negrita invasion. She called me at one in the morning to tell me this. "I looked it up for you," she said as Todd lay beside me, shaking his head in disbelief.

Just last week Lydia and I stood on the banks of a frozen Hudson River, where we found shredded pieces of a Bible. Bits of Psalms, the Book of Job fluttered in the wind, stuck to the snow. I picked up a torn and burned fragment and read her these words: "Ye shall travel to a distant land and will find nothing there and ye shall not return."

I'd laughed because it was a joke, but Lydia has never had much of a sense of humor. She foresees bad whereas I see good. Not good naively, but I just don't expect bad things will happen the way Lydia does. She has a grim view, and at times I wonder how it is possible we came from the same family. In her more cryptic moments, Lydia says we did not. "You take things too seriously, Lyd," I told her. That was the last thing I said to her before I left.

I've never had an airport all to myself before. The quiet is unsettling. Airports are noisy places, filled with the bustle of comings and goings. But here there are only distant sounds—

music, voices, footsteps. A television is on somewhere inside. I can hear a generic announcer's voice, shouting when a team scores, giving the play-by-play. The men in the back give brief cheers, break out in laughs.

The airport maintenance people arrive to wash the windows, scrub the floor. With squeegees the men rub the windows clean, making sweeping motions. They are meticulous in their task, careful to get every spot. I am impressed with their work as they reach high into the corners, coming down straight. No drips. Then they sweep the floor, making sure to get under my feet. Politely they ask me to raise my bags to the seat, which I do.

When the maintenance people leave, they lock the doors. For a long time I don't see anybody. There are things I would like to ask for. My head is throbbing but I have no water to take some aspirin. In the hours I've been sitting in this hard, plastic chair I've begun to have a longing for simple things—a bed, a home-cooked meal.

There is an art to keeping people waiting, and these bureaucrats have perfected it. It is nothing like keeping someone waiting in a doctor's office or at a bus stop. Because you know that eventually the doctor will take you, the bus will come. And I know that sooner or later they will explain to me what the problem is. But it feels as if they could keep me here forever, as if they have nothing but time.

In the middle of the night I am escorted into a small office where the colonel who is now overseeing my situation explains that they are trying to decide what to do with me. He is an unpleasant man with dead eyes. Eyes that never look anyone in the face. Eyes set on the paper in front of him. He has the kind of eyes that make you understand that one human being can actually pull out the fingernails of another.

He will not explain the problem, but refers to it as my "case." He says that they are looking into my case, never taking his gaze off the floor. He informs me that it is the decision of the head of customs that I will not be allowed entry into this country. He says that this has not been up to him. It comes from a place much higher up. I will be returned, he tells me, to my port of embarkation when the next flight leaves.

"And when will that be?" I ask in my best Spanish, my voice trembling. Though he will not look at me, I stare at his face. He has smooth skin, the color of olive oil, and his lips are fine and red. Perhaps if I cry, he will take pity on me. Or perhaps he won't.

"In six days, but we will make every effort to expedite your departure."

"And what will I do until my flight leaves?"

He shrugs. "That is being decided."

"Can you at least tell me what the problem is, sir?" I add *sir,* hoping this will make him think I am respectful and polite.

"No," he says, "I cannot." He suggests I take it up with their embassy when I am returned to my place of origin. I am surprised by this construction. One thinks of oneself as returning, but not of being returned. Lost keys, stray dogs, bodies are returned.

"Are you a journalist?" he asks.

"No," I tell him, "I am not a journalist." Of course, I am a journalist, of sorts. But I am not the kind that they should concern themselves with. A technicality that happens to be true, though probably they would consider it a lie.

By profession, I do updates for travel guides. Often my

updates take me to places where travelers' advisories are in effect. But the travelers' advisory has been in effect here for almost three decades, and it is the belief of my editors at Easy Rider Guides, the aging-hippie travel-guide service for which I work, that *la isla,* as the people who live here call it, will be opening up soon.

I've had my share of dubious assignments. Paying my dues, Kurt, my editor, calls it. I've wined and dined my way through the Czech Republic, feasting on potato stew. When the couple sent the postcard from Honduras to say that the ferry from La Ceiba to Roatán hadn't run in years, I was the one who was sent to find the rotting dock on the mosquito-infested coast to verify that, indeed, the ferry hadn't run in years. I did a five-day stint in Haiti last year (where I would have been happy to have never left the hotel) because my editor told me, You'll see, any day now, Haiti will be opening up too. All I saw were shantytowns, open sewers, and naked children playing in mud.

Certainly a country that is trying to promote its tourist industry shouldn't be detaining a woman who updates travel guides. If they'd just let me explain, they'd know how foolish this is. I could show them the checklist I have in my bag. I have to confirm that you can eat for under five dollars at El Colibrí or fly to Cayo Grande for twelve dollars. I have to rent a car and drive from one end of the island to the other and note all the places where you can use a coupon and get some gas, where you can buy a cheese sandwich.

Mostly I am to go to Puente de Juventud and visit the new joint-venture hotels being opened by Canadians and Swedes, sleep in the new beds, get copies of the activity sheets. Do they have banana-eating or beer-guzzling contests? Can you ride a glass-bottomed boat? I need to check on the snorkeling. See if they have a day camp, pony rides. Do kids under twelve eat free on the all-inclusive? How good are the security guards?

Now the colonel looks at me in such a way that I understand our conversation is over, but I don't want it to be. I want an explanation and, more than that, as I stand there shivering, I want a blanket. It seems like such a small thing, but it is suddenly so essential to me. I'm not sure how I'll make it through the night. Todd is the warm one, but I am cold. Even in the heat of summer, I need a cover over me. I hesitate, thinking better of it; then I ask if I could have a blanket, and the colonel looks at me with neither rage nor compassion. Rather, he looks at me with indifference. "This is not a hotel," he says.

I've noticed, I want to reply. But it seems better to say nothing at all. I think that at any moment he will mention Isabel. He'll say, "Why don't you tell about what happened the last time you were here." Instead he starts shuffling papers on his desk. "Anything else?" he asks abruptly.

"Yes, I have to go to the bathroom."

He signals to one of his guards. The stone-faced guard with a gun in his hand accompanies me down a narrow corridor. To my right is the bathroom and straight ahead is the door outside. It has been left ajar and a warm, tropical breeze blows in. I hesitate, smelling the salt, the sea, a hint of jasmine in the air, and for an instant I think I could dash through the opening into the night, but the guard motions with the butt of his rifle. The bathroom is gray and there is no mirror. There is also no toilet paper.

I am taken back to the immigration waiting room, where it appears I will be for a while. I try to stretch out across three plastic chairs, but the armrests press into my sides. Tossing a light jacket over my shoulders, I arrange myself better, resting on my duffel, the way I have seen pictures of travelers stranded by snowstorms in Denver, strikes in Milan, though I have never been a stranded traveler before this night.

Just when I feel as if I could doze off, as if I could actually sleep with my head resting on my palm, one of the guards, a pleasant enough man with a nice face, informs me that I am to be moved upstairs, where I'll be more comfortable. He hoists my duffel as I follow him up some winding steps into a departure lounge. The lounge, lined with vinyl-covered benches, smells of grease and beer and does not look like much of an improvement, except that the guard tells me I can stretch out on the benches. He also tells me that there are no more flights until Tuesday so I could actually live in this lounge until they find a flight for me.

I sit down, trembling. Though I have my duffel with me, the only warm things it contains are a few cotton sweaters, an extra pair of jeans. I pull on a sweater, but still my teeth chatter. Travel light, Todd told me, but take a sweatshirt. You never know, he said. He's practical about this sort of thing, but somehow I don't listen. My bag is heavy with a blow-dryer and a clothes steamer, but no sweatshirt. The windchill was fifteen below when I left home; I handed Todd my winter coat at the airport when I kissed him good-bye, knowing he'd be waiting at the same place upon my return.

I've never been very good at being awake when everyone else is asleep. At home I want to wake someone up to keep me company. I'm not one for cleaning drawers or counting sheep. When I was younger, I used to drink a little brandy, though I never felt right the next day. I try to lie down on the narrow benches, but as soon as I start to doze, I feel myself slipping toward the floor.

The fluorescent lights are on in the duty-free shops that line the departure lounge, and I get up and walk around. One shop displays a giant lizard, stuffed in attack position, and a weird chess set that appears medieval in origins. The pawns are belly dancers as if out of a harem; the rook is a real castle; the knight, a knight on his rearing horse. I wonder where this chess set came from and what it is doing at the duty-free shop in the Aeropuerto Internacional.

There is a display of wood carvings and giant spiders with wire legs that I try to envision on coffee tables in Munich and Amsterdam. Do these spiders really exist on *la isla?* There are ceramics—bowls that look as if they'd disintegrate with water in them, brittle-looking plates, perfect for hurling in domestic battles on Spanish-language soap operas, but I can't imagine serving food on them. The ceramics have squiggles and shapes on the sides in an attempt to appear indigenous, but the natives were wiped out centuries ago.

Books line the counter. Propaganda mostly. *The Revolution from Columbus to the Present. The Diary of a Guerrilla Fighter.* Leafing through a volume of contemporary poetry, I glance up and see the woman. She is lying flat on a shelf, her skin pasty white, her dark hair perfectly coiffured, red lipstick, a sheet pulled up to her chin. Slamming the book down, I dash back into the darkness, my hand pressed to my mouth, because I am certain she is dead. Then I notice that the airport is full of these women, lying on pallets, wrapped in sheets, on the floor. They are workers on the graveyard shift, but they all look dead. At any moment I expect them all to rise up. Overhead Muzak plays "Guantanamera." Innumerable flies

and mosquitoes buzz around my head; I swat blindly at the
air, slapping myself in the face.

As I stand here, I realize that it was in this room that I first
saw Isabel. Or rather first noticed Isabel, because my sense
was, even then, that I'd seen her before. But it was here in
this departure lounge that I noticed her darting eyes, caught
her furtive glance. I saw her the day I was departing on an
excursion to Puente de Juventud, the Bridge of Youth, a
beach resort twenty minutes' flight away. Manuel was waiting
with me in this same airport where I am being detained
when I noticed the young woman, close to my age. She was
hugging people who were leaving, greeting others who were
arriving. Her laughter echoed through the lounge and everyone seemed to know her, even the guards and officials.

The jeans she wore were too big and the navy blue sweater
was too heavy for the season. It seemed as if she was wearing
clothes borrowed from a man with whom she was intimate.
But it was her black eyes that caught me as they skitted from
person to person, from face to face. She gazed across doorways as if she was involved in contraband or some form of
espionage. I'd seen things like this at airports before. But she
seemed to be searching for someone she'd lost in the crowd.

It was Manuel who told me who she was. Of course, the
moment he told me, it was as if I had already known. Everyone who'd been to *la isla* knew who she was. And then he
said, If you like, I'll arrange for you to meet her. He was a
distant relation, a cousin by marriage, but they were the same
age and had grown up together. She likes to have visitors, he
said. As you know, he told me, though I didn't at the time,
for years she has been trying to leave.

My heart pounds in my chest. Once I captured a baby

rabbit in the woods and its heart beat this way in my palm. My mother said it died of fright. Now I curl up on the bench in a little ball, teetering on the edge. A driving rain falls, hitting the picture window. Outside three jumbo jets sit idle, waiting to take people away.

Two

THE POLICE CAR speeds along the outskirts of Ciudad del Caballo. Though it is a Monday afternoon, the beige, nondescript car does not need its siren because the streets are empty, as if everyone is asleep, as if they have decided to stay home. Teenagers ride bicycles in the middle of the road, ignoring what little traffic there is. A whole family rides on a single bicycle like a circus act. Dodging potholes, they wave as we pass.

We drive by shantytowns, tin-roofed shacks held together with plywood and cardboard. Small children race to the roadside, dirty faces staring at us. Shabby dogs and one-eyed cats stagger across the road. The sunlight is so intense that I have to shade my eyes. Major Lorenzo puts down the window and a blast of hot air blows into the backseat. Warmth seeps into my bones. "Perhaps that is too much wind?" he asks, but I tell him no, it feels good.

He drapes his arm across the seat where his driver sits. His nails are manicured, buffed. He wears a gold watch—a

Rolex—that shows the time to be just after noon. He and his driver, who is hidden behind reflector shades, exchange glances. Both men wear short sleeves that reveal sturdy, tanned forearms. "Are you hungry?" Major Lorenzo asks me. "Have you had something to eat?"

"I had breakfast," I answer, thinking of the hard roll and black coffee I'd been given at the airport. He nods, satisfied with my reply. Major Lorenzo—a small, compact man with a thin mustache and wire-rimmed glasses—has taken charge of my case. He seems somewhat embarrassed, sorry to put me through this. When he met me at the airport, he shook my hand.

He is a go-between, and someone else has given him his orders. In fact, it seems as if he is as ignorant of the details of my case as I am. Or else he is good at pretending. When I asked him if he could explain what the difficulty was, he said, "I am sorry, but I have not been informed. I am just taking care of . . . how do you say it, the red tape." He grinned when he found this expression. We both laughed, a hearty laugh that friends might share over a beer.

We drive swiftly now past the crumbling arches of colonial houses, some held up by ancient scaffolding. Others have no roofs. The frames of windows stand empty, open to the sky. They are taking me to the hotel where I will stay until I can be returned to where I came from. That is what I have been told. We turn right on to the Miramar, the wide road that follows the sea.

Along the sea there is a wall. Spray rises from it. I gasp as a young man dives off for his afternoon swim. On the Miramar, houses once owned by the rich stand with their fading crimson, sun-drenched yellow, cobalt blue facades in need of paint. In these houses ten families now live. We come to a red light but do not stop.

We turn, then zigzag down side streets, until we arrive at the main square. Major Lorenzo's aide opens my door, offering me a hand. His fingers on my arm are warm and sticky, and for the first time I notice that unlike Major Lorenzo he is wearing a gun. When he steps away, I pause in the bright sunlight, which burns hot on my face.

Tipping my head back, I gaze at the Hotel España. It is an old Spanish–style building with an arching portico, thick columns. Scarlet and yellow bougainvillea dangle from its balcony. A vine, the color of mangoes, climbs up the columns. Across the street in the main square people linger on benches, and I want to stroll down its crisscross paths, beneath the shade of its royal palms, but Major Lorenzo takes me gently by the arm, ushering me inside.

Everything in the lobby is wicker—white wicker—and the walls are painted white. There are creamy sofas and over-stuffed armchairs. Light pours in through the huge windows, which are open, as ceiling fans whirl, turning warm air. A woman sits in a fluffy chair, staring into space, probably waiting for someone who is late. Two Jamaican men in linen suits and red ties sit hunched over a pad of paper, smoking cigarettes.

Though I stayed here the last time, I hardly recognize the place now because it has been refurbished to meet the new demand in the tourist trade. Its dark, stuffy lobby has been replaced with all this wicker and light. It is a modest but decent hotel, one our guidebook only gives a brief mention to, short shrift really, but at a glance I think it is much better than the full-service ones we advise for tourists. This hotel lacks in modern conveniences (no air-conditioning or room service), but its floor and ceiling are now brightly decorated in mosaics in the old Spanish style. I will expand our entry on it during my stay.

Major Lorenzo asks if I want a view of the plaza. He tells me that from this room if I stand on my balcony I can see the sea. I think this is a very nice suggestion. The last time I was here I was given a room with a curtain across one wall. When I flung the curtain back, it revealed a brick wall.

It takes a long time for them to prepare my room. While I am waiting, I have a cup of coffee in the bar. I sit at a table and order a *café con leche* and toast, since it has been hours since I last ate. After the waiter takes my order, he doesn't leave. Instead he stands there, looking at me oddly. "You have been here before," he says, beaming. He is a tall man with wavy brown hair, and I recognize him as Enrique, the waiter who was grateful two years ago when I tipped him with toothpaste and cans of sardines, which is what people who visit *la isla* do. "So you have come back to see us once more," he says as we shake hands, introducing ourselves again.

"I couldn't stay away," I tell him, surprised at how this is true. Enrique was the one who told me to be careful when he saw me with Isabel. He tried to whisper something in my ear, but I don't like whispering. I never have and I didn't listen to what he said then and I suppose I would not listen again now. As he asks me how I have been, I wonder if he knows what has happened to me, but I don't mention it.

In the corner of the bar there is a pool table, where a group of blond men and two dark women are shooting. The sound of breaking balls shatters the quiet of the bar. I do not recall seeing a pool table when I was here the last time. A few

moments later the coffee arrives. It is watery and the milk
swirls in the cup. The toast is served dry. "There's no sugar,"
Enrique informs me, his face full of chagrin.

From the bar where I sip my coffee, I observe Major Lorenzo in the lobby, briefing a small group of staff. Waiters and
desk clerks keep glancing my way. The hotel is run by the
state, so all the staff are government workers, and they are
being informed of my plight. I guess there will be no guard
posted at my door; they won't need one. After a few moments Major Lorenzo comes to join me. Though I offer him
a seat, he remains standing. "I will be back later," he says,
"when I have some news. In the meantime you should make
yourself as comfortable as possible."

"I was wondering," I ask him, "if I couldn't just sit out
front in the plaza where there are trees."

"No," he says firmly, "that will not be possible." Then he
pauses, gazing down at me. "But the hotel is at your disposal," he says. "Do you understand?"

"Yes, I think I understand."

"Good, it is important that we understand each other."
Then he smiles and heads for the door. "So I will see you this
afternoon. Hopefully I'll have some news."

As he is leaving, I think I have forgotten something in his
car, but as I run to the door to call him, several hotel atten-
dants stand in my way.

Returning to my table at the bar, I look around. I had
expected interrogations, cinder-block rooms, not the mo-
saic-trimmed lobby of this hotel, not doormen in white suits
blocking my way. Perhaps they do not know about Isabel.
Perhaps they know nothing about what happened between
us, and they are detaining me just because I worked as a

journalist on a tourist's visa, something *la isla* cannot abide. It has nothing to do with Isabel after all.

Still I cannot sit here and not imagine her rushing through this lobby in her pale flowing skirt, her body that seemed to be swimming through air, her dark hair tied back in a bun, the white silk blouse under which she wore no bra. I can see all the heads turning, hear the whispers. Everyone knew who she was. And of course that was part of it. She wanted them to.

At the table across from me two Finnish men, one of whom is a dwarf, and an elderly German in green polyester pants are buying drinks for three local women. A pretty young woman in a red dress gets up, tugging on her dress, but the dwarf pulls her down into his lap. He has pudgy, gnarled hands and he runs them up and down her arms. He stuffs money into her bodice and she laughs, pushing him away. The elderly man is fondling another woman, who has a sour look on her face. She ogles a tall blond man, probably from Scandinavia, who just arrived, sporting a large backpack.

One of the women has a child with her—a toddler with golden Afro curls who eats candy bar after candy bar. A few moments after I sit down, this woman gets up. She leaves the hotel on the arm of the elderly German, the child chasing after her.

They have given me a room that overlooks the square. It has a small balcony from which I really can see the sea, twin beds, and a television that gets the Caribbean equivalent of MTV. The first thing I do when I get to the room is open the French doors to let in the light and air. Noise from the street rises to my window. I can hear the voices of schoolchildren at play.

Jessica would be having lunch now. A bologna sandwich on white bread, an orange, animal crackers. The same thing every day. Todd probably let her wear whatever she wanted to school—the Aladdin sweatshirt, the dinosaur skirt, lace stockings. When I am away, Todd has many weak moments when it comes to Jessica. He buys her Barbie dolls; he doesn't say no to candy as a snack. I am the strict one, the one who lays down the rules.

My daughter is five and I've left her at home. She prefers it there, with her dog, her yard, her friends. She has a nightlight with a rainbow that she cannot sleep without. Todd and I have this understanding: I can go on these junkets three or four times a year and in this way get my taste of freedom. My fix, he calls it. It's enough to keep me going. And this didn't seem such a bad idea, to come here in January during the worst part of the winter. Even Todd thought it was a good idea.

I've always needed a secret life. Diaries with locks, hiding places under the stairs. When I was a teenager, I snuck out to meet boys my father forbade me to see on darkened street corners, just blocks from my house. I slid down the drainpipe. Getting back in was harder, but the boys hoisted me onto the roof. When I make love to Todd, I think of things I shouldn't think of. Other men, women. I imagine myself in different places. Distant lands are foreign bodies to me, perfect for clandestine affairs. I require these small absences. Time away. Todd accepts this, though he doesn't know why. He doesn't want to know. If I start to tell him, he walks out of the room.

When I go on these junkets, I do pretty much what I want. That is, whatever happens, happens, and we don't talk about it. Not that so much has ever happened. I've had a few

late-night rumbas, a groping hand or two. Moonlight infatu-
ations at tourist resorts when I grow weary of my checklist;
scenic walks can grow tedious alone. But what I really like is
to rent a car and drive around a place where I've never been.
Outside of Prague I went from castle to castle. The last time I
was here, I rolled down the windows and drove across the
country and back. I only stopped for gas and to drink orange
juice at roadside stands.

It's not that Todd can't get away; it's that he doesn't want
to. He doesn't like to be away from what he knows. I don't
really fault him for this, though I wish it wasn't so. But Todd
is content, playing suicide—a game whose name confounds
me and rules defy me—with Jessica in the backyard, or skat-
ing in the park. For a hobby he repairs the gas streetlamps on
our block, but mainly he is an architect and a good one at
that, and despite the recession he has work in the office, jobs
he says he can't afford to lose.

It's not that I blame Todd for what has happened. It is just
that if he had come with me—if he wanted to come when I
travel for my updates—then I wouldn't have met Manuel. If I
hadn't met Manuel, I would never have met Isabel. Or
rather, I might have seen Isabel, but I would not have known
who she was. And then I wouldn't be here.

I met Manuel a few days into my first visit to the island, at
the bar of the Hotel Miramar. I had come to sample the
malted milks, which I was told were the best on *la isla*, and to
visit the old casinos, untouched since the days of Meyer
Lansky, who had built a few here. Once renowned for its
posh backroom gambling and spectacular vistas, for its high-
stakes poker and call girls with blue-black hair, the Miramar
is now known for its malted milks and its peeling murals of
almond-eyed girls bent back in the arms of swarthy men.

Manuel was sitting at the table across from mine. In front of him an ashtray was heaped with butts of Marlboros, one of them still burning. He nursed a glass with a faint brown liquid in it and tapped his foot to the tune of "Sueño Tropical," an old Pico Rodríguez hit from the fifties. Everything about him seemed to be moving. His fingers, his feet. He beat his hands on the table as if playing the bongos, though the rhythm he tapped out had nothing to do with the music.

After watching me for a few moments, Manuel picked up his drink and walked over to my table. He was a small man with a compact frame, and long white fingers, which I noticed as he pulled back the chair with a single movement, inquired if he could sit down, and seated himself. "Do you have anything to sell?" he asked—jeans, watches, toothpaste, nail polish, canned food, soap.

As he leaned forward, his open shirt revealed a chest of coarse hair. His smile made all his features turn upward as he asked if I wanted to change money. I replied no and told him I had only come here to update a travel guide, and he said, "That's too bad." He had come to the Miramar, as many people do, to look out to sea. He told me, joking over a rum collins, that he was waiting for his ship to come in—the one that would literally take him away. He said, if I wanted, he'd show me around.

I unpack. It is important to get organized, to put things in their places. To know where everything is. The few dresses I've brought are wrinkled, but they'll straighten out in the closet or freshen up with my steamer. I check my case of adaptor plugs, tuck blouses and T-shirts into a drawer.

Then I take a shower, spending a long time, letting the warm water course across my body. I'm in the shower so long that I find myself staring at the shower curtain. It is an old plastic curtain with herds of antelope bounding across it, heading for pine groves.

As I am drying my hair, it occurs to me that there are no antelopes on *la isla*; no pine trees either. Palmettos and, once, parrots, yes; even pirates and buried treasure. But antelope and deciduous pine, no. These are northern scenes, from latitudes above, so I can only assume that—like the cars and the TVs and the airplane I came on—the shower curtain is Soviet-made, circa 1960.

I stand on the balcony, brushing my thick, damp hair, the color of pennies, which takes forever to dry in the humid breeze. In the plaza below children play with hoops. Men in lime green and eggshell blue guayaberas sit on benches, smoking cigarettes. A black woman passes, dressed in spotless white. Her dress clings to her basketball buttocks, her torpedo breasts, and the men turn their heads and start whooping. One of them applauds, but the woman in white doesn't turn around.

My gaze follows her as she disappears into the old city. Two years ago I walked with Isabel through those winding streets, where I first saw the dogs, roaming, glancing our way as they vanished down dark alleyways. She looped her arm through mine as we were heading to dinner.

Inside the houses, we saw women with their hair in curlers who stood ironing in front of the blue light of the television. Every house has a television, Isabel told me—the gift of the revolution to each household. Every couple gets a television when they marry; every woman gets an extra rationed nightgown. She gets another one when she is pregnant, which the women joke are the only two times in her life that a woman doesn't need a nightgown.

As we strolled the cobblestone streets, I peered into the open doorways as the women ironed school uniforms for the next day—small girls' light blue dresses, boys' navy blue shirts. Teenagers danced to rock videos. There were never any lights on. They were not allowed. But they could watch television and they could iron. The mothers never looked up as they concentrated on their careful, even strokes. On the television there is only one station, and after the news and sports, after the music videos, there is always the same late-night program: El Caballo expounding on the recent achievements of the regime.

Walking through the old city, where hookers beckoned from alleyways, Isabel grimaced as we listened to the voice of the leader, and it seemed as if he were speaking from every corner, from every house we passed, and I felt Isabel's arm tighten around mine, trembling.

Three

ISABEL never sees her father, Manuel told me after I noticed her at the airport. She does not speak to him. They
do not say hello when they are in the same room, but he will
not let her go. You know, it is said that he has sixteen sons,
but she is the only girl. Except for one boy, they are all
bastards, just like our leader is a bastard. Seventeen children,
you know. *¡Qué cojones!* Manuel puffed up his chest like a
rooster. Our leader, he told me, never sleeps in the same bed
two nights in a row.

He tried to arrange for me to meet with Isabel, "But you
know, she is very busy." Somehow I sensed she did not want
to meet me. Or that he did not really want me to meet her.
Whatever it was, I knew I probably would not see Isabel
again, and it didn't matter that much to me. I might catch
glimpses of her at the airport or in bars, but meeting her,
after all, was a digression. An interesting diversion, but not
really a part of my reason for being here.

I went about my business, checking out the snorkeling on

a remote strip of beach called Smuggler's Cove, renowned for its reef. There I tiptoed across oily sand and cast-off debris to swim above undulating beds of sea urchins. The beach bar had been long closed. Smuggler's Cove would receive a small correction in my update.

In the city a few days later Manuel accompanied me as I visited the Monuments of the Revolution. He led me slowly past the small, unlit cases of the Museum of the History of the Revolution, which begins its history not with the great liberator of *la isla*, as you might expect, but with the arrival of the first Spanish ship in 1472. They docked for a night and dropped off the first white man to live on *la isla*—Alejandro Martínez, a Spanish sailor, believed to be a Moor. He was missing his right hand and the fingers on his left, his nose, and his ears. The Taino Indians knew a holy man when they saw one and left him alone to forage and live in a cave in the hills.

For years Martínez lived in seclusion, walking the perimeters of the island, until he determined its shape to be that of a crocodile and named it Caimán, after its shape. When his solitude became too much, Martínez began to greet the ships that stopped to dock there. At first they were afraid of him, but the word soon spread across the high seas that a man known for his seclusion and torment lived on an unnamed island in the turquoise sea. The sailors, too, determined he was a holy man. They brought him gifts of seeds from coffee plants and avocado trees, they brought him kittens and dogs, goats and horses, and Martínez bred these and filled the island—which had once been merely a place of parrots and howler monkeys and snakes—with the domestic animals of his own country.

When Columbus came, he killed all the Taino Indians,

whom he called Carib, after the old Spanish word for canni-
bal. One Taino woman, it was said, escaped to the cave
where Martínez lived and eventually became his wife.
Martínez watched this slaughter from his hiding place in the
hills, but he could read and he could write and he recorded
all that he saw in a book entitled *The Conquest of the Tainos on
the Island of the Caimán*. Except for Bernal Díaz del Castillo's
The Conquest of Mexico, it is the only definitive portrait that
we know of an ancient people and their massacre.

From the time of Columbus the islands and its sea and the
people who came to live there became known as the Caribbean, and for four hundred years the Spanish ruled *la isla*.
They brought with them tobacco and sugarcane. They also
brought with them slaves whose ships carried spiders the size
of fists that nestled in the banana groves, and rats and snakes
and cholera.

At the end of the nineteenth century a Spanish landowner,
Andrés Ortiz, freed his slaves and indentured servants and led
them into the hills and the rain forest to begin *la isla*'s first
war of liberation. The Americans would join Ortiz and his
growing squadrons in what came to be known as the War of
Liberation from Spain. When the victory was complete, the
American Marines at the *fortaleza* were told to fly the flag of
the liberation. They flew the Stars and Stripes instead.

More than fifty years later a lone soldier would flail about
in the hills with his band of followers, fighting a protracted
guerrilla war. He would crawl, holding his breath, through
burning fields of sugarcane, set afire to smoke him out. No
one really knew who he was or where he came from, and
rumor spread that he was the first Spaniard and his Taino
wife. That he was born of a holy man and a martyr as well.
But in truth this soldier who they came to call El Caballo was

the bastard son of a Spanish peasant who ran a *finca* in the eastern provinces.

He would spend years in prison, where this man famed for his incessant speaking—for keeping his brothers and fellow soldiers up all night—would never speak, and his guards came to refer to him as El Mudo, the Mute. And eventually he would become president of the republic, chairman of the Socialist Party, prime minister, director of the congress, and head of the armed forces. And on the day he became president, the flag of *la isla* flew in the wing-shaped harbor of Puerto Angélico for the first time.

After our visit to the museum, where I made notes for the "Brief History" section of the guide, Manuel invited me out for pizza. We stood in a line that snaked around the block, in which old women in cotton dresses with aprons shifted from hip to hip, arms akimbo. "You see," he said, "once we had hopes; now we have lines." Children dashed up and down the line as their mothers called to them. Men who looked bored leaned against the wall as the line inched forward. When at last we purchased a greasy slab of bread with cheese running off it, Manuel said, "Everything here makes me sick. Why do tourists want to come? All we want to do is leave."

We wandered over to the seawall to eat our pizza. On the way he did a little mambo step, a spin on his heels. The wall was populated with young couples—girls in school uniforms sat as boys in work clothes arched their groins into their girlfriends' backs. Others nestled, arm-in-arm, sleeping on each other's shoulders. Manuel and I sat, swatting the flies and eating our lumpy pizza. Oil slid down my wrist.

"You aren't working today?" I asked him.

He shook his head. Because of rationing, there was no

electricity in his office and he could not use the computer. This happened about three times a week. So really there was no sense for him to go to work more than a day or two a week. "So I come here," he told me, "and watch the sea."

Manuel worked as a statistician in the Ministry of Agriculture. "I know it sounds impressive," he said, "but what I actually do is fix numbers so they add up right. Per capita necessities, labor hours, production costs, profits. The goal of my job is to make it look as if we are ahead. Of course, we will never be ahead, but I just need to make the numbers look as if we are."

Manuel shrugged and smiled, which made his whole face turn upward like a child's picture of a smiling sun. It's not that hard, he said, to make the numbers look right. It also helped him to know what the shortages are, and if he knows what the shortages are, he can anticipate them. And this is good for black-market sales.

"The black market is about the only thing I can count on." Then Manuel began to complain about everything. He complained about the food he could not eat, about his pointless jobs and dead-end love affairs, the synthetic fabric in his clothing, the lines in which he had to wait to buy rum, the furniture he wanted to order from catalogs, the things he couldn't afford, the heart medicine he needed for his mother, the CD player he wanted for himself.

We took a long sweaty walk along the seawall, where hordes of children banged against my thighs, begging for pencils and Chiclets. These I carried in abundance, and so as in the Pied Piper the children followed us for blocks until Manuel shooed them away.

When we stopped in a small tourist restaurant for lemonade, the waiter asked Manuel what he was doing inside a restaurant and asked to see his papers, but I convinced the waiter that Manuel was my guide. The waiter did not see Manuel take my hand and press it to his lips. Nor did he see me pull away as I told Manuel that I was married and my husband and daughter were waiting for me at home. Manuel shrugged with a laugh. "So what does that matter?" he asked. "Here we live in the present tense."

"You have no one . . . ?" I asked.

"My wife and son left ten years ago. I was supposed to join them, but it just didn't happen."

"I'm sorry . . ."

"It's the boy I miss. I'm surprised at how much I do. He's thirteen now and I wouldn't recognize him in the street." Then he sipped his lemonade in silence until the straw slurped at the bottom of the glass.

When we returned to my hotel, Isabel was sitting at a small table with a group of sorrowful women who emitted the odor of funeral flowers. They were dressed in spandex bodysuits; their jewelry clanged and their eyebrows were painted on. They were laughing as if someone had just told a very good joke. Isabel wore a pink cotton shift that made her look like a waif, as if she could just float away. She was laughing with them, smoking cigarettes. Of course, she must have known that they were whores. Certainly they knew who she was. When she saw us, she stood up. "Manuel, what a surprise! What are you doing here?" She kissed him on both cheeks.

She motioned for me to sit beside her, and someone pulled up a chair. When I sat down, she touched my hand, and I was startled by the coldness of her touch. "So," she said, "tell me: What have you seen? Manuel, you have been giving her the tour?" Then she tossed her head back and laughed as if this was a wonderful joke. Her bony hand pressed on mine, sending a shiver through me. In her cotton dress, I could see how thin she was. I could easily wrap my fingers around her wrist. A cup of coffee sat in front of her and a cigarette burned in the ashtray. "Museums," I told her.

"Oh, yes," she said, in a voice filled with irony. "We have many museums." She sighed, looking at me, and I looked back at her. "Museums and cigar factories. And, of course, our plastic-surgery hospitals. Have you seen any of our churches? The Church of the Apparitions—Manuel, you must take her there. Of course," she said with a wave of her hand, "this is the biggest apparition of all." She said this in English and the two of us laughed together. Manuel and the whores grinned dumbly, having missed the punch line.

Her skin was as white as if she'd never been in the sun, and she smelled faintly of cheap, imported perfume. Nina Ricci. At the airport I had only seen her in a crowded room, but now, sitting beside her, I saw something I had not seen before. I suppose that in a country where people are not free to speak, the eyes tell all. Though her frail bones and gaunt features weren't unusual on an island where there is so little food, the hungry look in her eyes startled me.

But beyond the raw-bone features, the distracted glance, I looked into the dark hollow of those eyes and saw a sadness I'd never seen before. Once I did some small-town reporting and I saw sad things, believe me. But this woman had a different kind. You could drop pebbles down, and they would never reach the bottom of that sadness.

"So," Isabel said, speaking in Spanish once again, "are you enjoying yourself? Have you gotten a good sense of how we live?" The prostitutes snickered and looked away.

"I've only just arrived," I replied.

Now she clutched my wrist and her skin was soft, but I wondered how a person could have cold hands in such a hot place and I thought this must be what a dead person feels like. "Look," she said, "you must come to see me." She scribbled her address on a slip of paper. "Come tomorrow," she said, pressing the slip of paper into my hands. "You must."

Four

THE HOTEL is at your disposal, Major Lorenzo said, and I have taken him at his word. I spend my first few hours acclimating to the place. Seeing what I can do with my time. There is a rooftop terrace where I can sun on plastic lounge chairs in the afternoon and drink rum-and-Cokes from four o'clock on or stay for the pig and lamb roast in the evening, when they set up the stereo with speakers that blast salsa, mostly pirated from Miami, across the rooftops of Puerto Angélico, the name by which the inhabitants still refer to it.

In the lobby there is the bar open twenty-four hours a day where prostitutes and tourists mingle and there is the restaurant open during meals. I can get my nails done or have a touch-up for about five dollars U.S., eat a plate of spaghetti, and shop at the tourist *tienda*. I wonder how much of my update I can do by phone, though Kurt would probably fire me if he knew.

Easy Rider Guides won't accept a tourist brochure as gospel. I have three walking tours to do—old Puerto Antonio, the Miramar where the castle is, and the Monuments of the Revolution. I have done these before, but Easy Rider wants me to do them again. I've argued that a five-hundred-year-old colonial fortress probably hasn't changed much in the last two years, but Easy Rider wants it all checked out—the walking tours, the dates of historic churches, the costs of meals on the budget plan, if all-inclusive includes sports equipment and snorkel gear. It makes a big difference to people if they have to rent everything they need. After all, a package is a package, and à la carte is à la carte.

But it looks now as if any work I get done will be from the lobby of this hotel, so I order a cup of coffee, which Enrique brings right away. He looks at me as if he wants to say something, but he seems to think better of it. As he turns to wait on another table, I think to myself that he must know the circumstances under which I am here. I take a few sips, but the coffee is tepid and weak. With a sigh, I sit back, gazing around the room, thinking how empty it feels.

This is a room where Isabel and I sat many times. It is one of the places where we made our plan. So it is odd to be here and know that she is gone. I have not heard from her in these past two years. Every day I've thought that the phone will ring, a letter will arrive. I will receive word. But I never have. Somehow I thought she would get word to me of her whereabouts, but it is as if she has fallen off the face of the earth, evaporated into thin air, and I almost believe she has. And that she planned it this way.

I take a few more sips of the coffee, then put the cup down. There isn't that much to do in this hotel except sit at the bar and sit on the roof. I opt for my room and decide to try and make phone calls from there. First I call Todd. To my surprise the connection goes right through. I hear the answering machine with Jessica's voice on the other end. "Hello, we can't come to the phone . . ." I've never really listened to my daughter's voice on the message, but now it sounds tentative and unsure, as if she is doing something that embarrasses her, as if we've pushed her too far. Jessica begged to let us put her voice on the answering machine, and then when we let her, she was so shy. Her voice seems brittle, as if it could break.

The answering machine cannot accept a collect call so the operator tells me I must call back. Instead I give her my father's number. I'm not sure why I call him, but I do. I could call Lydia, but she'd never accept the charges. Or she'd just freak out.

In two rings my father answers. When he hears it is from me and I am calling collect, he accepts, though not without hesitating, and asks in his gruff voice where and how I am. His voice is heavy, as if he's been asleep. CNN is in the background and for a moment I try to catch the news, to hear what disaster he is listening to, as if this can somehow bring me back to what I left behind.

When I hear his voice, my hands start to shake, not because he is my father, though there is some of that, but because I am sure someone is listening in. Why would it have taken so long to prepare this spartan room? Looking around at the twin beds that have only sheets on them and four little towels in the bathroom, I see that there was so little to prepare.

"Daddy, I can't really talk. I just wanted you to know that the weather is bad," I tell him, glancing out at the clear, blue skies, "and I'll be coming home soon."

"Oh," he says, "I'm sorry to hear that. It's nice here. Very warm; lots of sun." Since my mother's death he has lived in a condo near Sarasota. His apartment is somewhat inland and it is very muggy there. Once he saw an alligator, jaws spread, in a ditch by the side of the road. He is dating a woman whom Lydia and I have never seen nor spoken to, whom he refers to as Flo.

"Well, where I am the climate is bad."

"So that means you'll be coming home sooner than you planned?"

"That's right, Daddy. Will you call Todd and leave a message? Ask him to phone me."

"I'm not sure how the weather can be bad there and nice here. Do you think it's coming this way?"

"I don't think so, Daddy. Listen, I can't talk anymore. Tell Todd I'll be home sooner than I expected. And tell him not to worry, but to call me, okay?" I hang up, wondering if my father made any sense out of our conversation. My guess is that he did not.

When I go downstairs, Manuel is nursing a Red Stripe at the bar. He looks smaller than I remember him and seems heavier, though he still has a lightweight boxer's build. I have no idea how he knew he'd find me here, because I never told him that I was coming. And I'm not even sure how he got into the hotel, since the natives aren't allowed in the tourist hotels, but he is sitting there. He looks up and nods and I know that he's been expecting me.

Five

ISABEL'S APARTMENT was in the Miramar section, one of the nicer parts of town. But her street was blocks from the sea. Only a little breeze blew on this inland road and the air felt heavy and dusty. The front of the house, which had once been painted lemon yellow, was ensconced in a tangle of vines, bougainvillea that hadn't been cut back in years, liana that threatened to engulf it. The air was thick with the smell of overripe fruit, and from deep within the tangle, blood red orchids and scarlet mariposa bloomed.

I trod carefully across a lawn that was mostly weeds and mud with a few greenish brown patches of sod. Holding back the dead thickets, I made my way to the stone path, where thorns snagged at my legs. It was hot and as I walked through the arching foliage, I thought this must have once been a beautiful garden, cared for and tended, but now it had gone to ruin.

When I rang the bell, I waited for what seemed like a long time. Then footsteps clicked across the floor. A woman with clear blue eyes, almond skin, and wavy brown hair flecked with gray opened the door. She wore a trim white dress and smelled of gardenia, making me wish I hadn't worn my gray slacks and beige shirt. Though she was perhaps in her sixties, her features were fine, her skin smooth, and I was startled to find such beauty behind the maze of vines and thorns.

"I'm sorry to disturb you," I told her as she opened the door, "but Isabel asked me to stop by."

"I am Rosalba Calderón," she introduced herself, clasping my hand, "Isabel's mother. But she isn't here." Rosalba looked nothing like Isabel and only then did I realize that Isabel looked like her father—the one they called El Caballo, the Horse. I had not noticed it at the time when I first met her because she was so thin.

"Oh," I said, uncertain of what to do, "she asked me to come."

Rosalba looked confused, as if she was trying to remember something. "Oh, yes, I'm sure she mentioned that she was expecting you, but she's out right now." Then she smiled, pulling me into the dark, cool shadows of her vestibule. "Anyway, please, come in. She'll be here soon."

"Here, I brought you these." I handed Rosalba the bag of chocolates, peanut butter, and silk stockings that Manuel had told me to bring, and she quickly looked inside. "Ah," she exclaimed, "I love chocolate. And I love visitors, especially from other countries. We see people from away so rarely now."

Taking my hand, she led me through a small courtyard where the terra-cotta planters had no plants, past an ancient fishbowl filled with water and bits of coral and a plastic palm but no fish. No songbird had sung in the wrought-iron bird-cage for years; instead a wilted geranium, its yellowed leaves in need of pruning, sat inside. We climbed stairs, then passed through a large doorway where the wooden door stood ajar and entered a room whose darkness was in such contrast to the harsh sunlight outside that I stood blinded for a moment.

As my eyes adjusted, I felt the coolness of shuttered rooms. Smells were striking in their absence—no pots cooking on the stove, no lavender perfumes. Only a faint odor of old tobacco, as if a man had long ago lived within these walls. In the entryway was a portrait of a woman in an eggshell blue dress, pinched at the waist, her soft brown hair flowing over her shoulders. The eyes were the color of the dress she wore and I knew that this was a portrait of the woman who led me, painted some forty years before, when she was infamous throughout *la isla* for her love affair with a soldier, renowned for his virility, for his thirst for power, and for not sleeping in the same bed two nights in a row.

Rosalba led me through a maze of buckets. Holes in the ceiling revealed a bright blue sky. The buckets were half-filled with collected pools of rain; algae grew along the rims. With the shades drawn, the rooms were dim, except for the light that came through these holes in the roof. "Isabel," she said, "has been very busy and preoccupied these days with her career as a fashion model." It surprised me, but I could envision this gaunt, sad woman working as a fashion model.

"Oh, I didn't know . . ."

"Yes, she's in all the fashion magazines. You didn't think we had fashion magazines, did you?"

"No, I didn't."

"Well, we do and Isabel is in them quite frequently. She hopes to be going to Paris next year to model the spring line." This seemed odd since Manuel had told me that Isabel could not get a visa to leave, but I thought it best not to say anything because Rosalba seemed so proud of her daughter's achievements.

Rosalba paused in the living room, which was furnished with a wooden settee and cane armchairs that appeared to be hand-carved and very old, and she made a gesture as if she wanted me to sit down. I saw that the armrests were carved into lions and dragons, but the seats were hollow, devoid of their cane. "Shall we sit?" Rosalba said, wrapping her fingers around the wooden frame, as I gazed into the empty center of the chairs.

"Oh, not here." She laughed. "On the patio. We never sit here anymore." But neither of us moved. "My grandparents brought this furniture with them from Spain," she said, stroking the wood. "My grandmother died on the passage and my grandfather arrived with just my mother and these chairs. They lived in this house as I did when I was a girl. You used to be able to sit on them on this porch and smell the sugarcane burning across the Miramar. There was nothing but banana groves and tobacco and sugarcane fields here when I was small." She extended her hand toward a neighbor's house of battered walls and peeling paint.

"The first time El Caballo came to this house," Rosalba said, as she led me to the kitchen, "he sat in these chairs." She made us a tray of lemonade and two glasses that did not match and carried the clattering tray down the stairs and onto the patio. Motioning for me to sit, she poured the lemonade into the glasses. When he came to see me, Rosalba went on, the chairs had their cane. And my mother was a young widow and I was just a girl. He could as easily have become her lover as mine. You cannot imagine what he was like when I first met him. He was the biggest man I had ever seen. Here on *la isla* the men, except for the Africans, are not known for their size. But he was huge and he had those piercing dark eyes.

But what drew me to him wasn't any of this. It wasn't any of the things you'd think. I won't talk about him in bed, but it wasn't that either. It was the way he talked, it was what he said. He just looked you square in the face and he talked. Or he listened. His gaze made you feel as if you were the only person in the world and there was nowhere else that he ever had to be, though, of course, especially for El Caballo, this was hardly true.

My father died in a boating accident when I was six. A storm at sea. His body was never recovered and some people suspect that in fact there was no drowning, but that he escaped to another island and another life. Years ago I heard a rumor that he was living on Saint Lucia with a black woman from Mozambique. But whatever the real story was I never saw him again after I was six and I never had a man sitting across from me, listening to what I had to say.

So when El Caballo sat across from me, leaning forward and looking at me with that fixed gaze, I would just open up to him, more than I ever did with anyone, more than I ever did with him in bed. Stories poured out of me about my grandmother who was buried at sea and my father who was lost at sea, about my bereft grandfather who rode across the cane fields from dawn until dusk, and about my mother whose solitude only matched my own.

He was just a bookkeeper then who had come to help my mother with her accounts, but there was something about him, I must say, that made me believe he would do more than just balance our books. And in his own way he has. He has done what he set out to do. You must admire him for that, for whatever else he may have done. He was a dozen years older than I, but that did not matter. I knew him as well as I knew myself. We would still be together today, but, you see, in the end there were things we could not forgive.

He was gone for many years. When he returned, I was a grown woman, married to a prominent physician, and we had a young daughter. But I could not keep El Caballo away. Not that I wanted to. In fact, all my life I have never wanted him to stay away.

I never knew when he was coming, but I would listen for the car in low gear without its lights on that would pull up in front of the big house by the sea where I lived with my husband. When it became too difficult for us to meet in my home, we rented a small apartment in the center of town. Our love nest. Whenever I could I went there and waited for him to come. Some days he did and some days he did not. While I waited for him, sometimes I decorated or cleaned, but mainly I read—mostly history and the biographies of great men. I read until the cabinets and shelves of the little apartment were filled, dreaming that someday I would be in a book someone wrote about him. It seemed that I was always waiting for him. And probably I still am.

Whenever my husband was out of town, I left our daughter, Serena, with my mother and stayed with El Caballo in the little apartment. He was a restless sleeper, up half the night, smoking cigars, drinking white rum. Fitful. He was always going to the window, looking out, coming back to bed, turning on the light.

I am a sound sleeper, but when he was with me I could feel the bed rise and fall. One night, I don't know what it was, he fell asleep hard and for almost the entire night he did not move. Suddenly, near dawn, he woke with a jolt as if something had startled him. He sat up and had difficulty catching his breath.

I opened the windows wide to let in the air. He asked for water and I brought it to him. Then he told me his dream. He said he saw himself as a horse, beautiful, sleek, galloping across an open field. He watched himself racing across fields, until it occurred to him that he couldn't stop. All night long, he said, he'd ridden on and on because he knew that when he did stop he would be dead. He was frightened then. He told me, Rosa—that was what he always called me, Rosa—I can never stop.

Recently there have been rumors of illness. Talk of colon cancer, rare diseases of the blood. But the people call him a *bicho malo*—a bad bug who will live to be very old. We have been apart for over thirty years, but I know that he will come back to me. People say he won't, but someday he will. I think he will come back when it is time for him to die.

For years now, she said, I have hardly seen him, but it is as if I know where he is, what he is doing every day. And, of course, there is Isabel. My daughter, you know, she is everything to me. Serena went to America long ago and Isabel is all that I have left. I cannot look at her and not think of him.

The shadows of the day were growing long when Rosalba finally rose. "Well," she said, "I've just gone on and on. Really, it's so unlike me." She went to the edge of the patio and peered at the road. "I can't imagine what's keeping my daughter. It's so rude of her, if she told you to come, not to call."

"It's all right. Probably she was delayed. Or maybe she just forgot . . ."

"I worry about her. Here I've gone on and on, but I know nothing about you. Do you have a child?"

"Yes, I do . . ."

"Well, then you know what it is. To worry about someone so."

"You can't really ever forget or get away when you have a child, can you?" I asked.

Rosalba looked up at me sadly. "Oh, some people can." She poured the last of the warm lemonade into my glass as darkness settled over the holes in the roof of the house. The absence of cooking smells brought a despair over me, as heavy as the one within those walls.

"My life," Rosalba said, with a tinge of remorse, "would have been completely different if I hadn't had her. But, of course, I can't imagine my life without her. If she could just get along with her father, I wouldn't worry so. The problem with them, you know, is that they are so much alike."

When I left, no taxi could be found. Though I was only a few miles from the center of town, no buses came there either. Rosalba had to bribe a neighbor to drive me to the Miramar, where I found a taxi driver who for five dollars would take me to my hotel. I asked him to take the Miramar though it was longer because I wanted to be close to the water. Opening my window, I breathed in deeply. Spray moistened my arm. In the distance out to sea I could see a gathering storm.

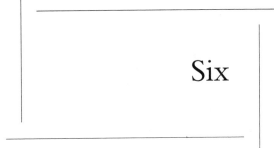

Six

MANUEL says I look well and healthy with my tan. He leans against the barstool, dressed in a blue T-shirt and jeans. He asks if I have been island-hopping, but I tell him that my tan comes from a half hour on the Hotel España roof deck. *La isla*, I tell him, was to be my only stop. I ask how it is that he knows I am here, but he says he didn't know. This is just one of his haunts. I eye him suspiciously and then he offers, "Word gets around."

I tell him that I have had some problems with immigration and I am not allowed to leave the hotel. That, in fact, I am being deported in the next few days, and he doesn't look very surprised.

"Have they told you what they think you've done?"

"They haven't told me a thing." I ask him what he thinks the problem is and he shrugs. "Do you think it's because of Isabel?"

He shrugs. "Who knows? It could be because of anything," he says.

Manuel and I make a plan. He will return the next evening and have dinner with me. In the meantime he will try to talk with some people to see if this can't be cleared up. I ask him if I should contact Rosalba and he presses his lips together. "Let me think about that," he says. "We'll figure a way out of this mess."

He kisses me on the cheek when he leaves, pressing my hand. "You still look great, baby; you really do."

"Have you . . . have you heard from her?" I gather the nerve to ask him after all.

"Oh, sure, from time to time. You know, messages get through. She's fine. She's living in Spain."

"Spain?"

"Yes. She likes it there."

I go back upstairs to my room and try Todd again. He answers on the first ring. I can't talk, I tell him, but try to understand. The weather is not good, the climate is bad. If I can, I'm going to Jamaica.

"Is the weather any better there?" he asks. Then he pauses as if something has just occurred to him. "Maggie, are you all right?"

"Yes, I'm fine. Or at least I think I am."

He clears his throat the way Todd does when he's starting to get concerned. "What does that mean? Is there some kind of trouble? Is something wrong?"

"I can't tell you now. I wish I could . . ." I think maybe I will tell him, but there is a loud crackling sound and the line goes dead.

Seven

I IMAGINE Isabel writing from a village in Spain: *On the island where I come from, we have the smallest beasts. A frog that will rest on your fingernail. A mammal no bigger than a thimble that looks like a shrew. The pygmy owl a child can cup in his fist. And the zunzuncito, the world's smallest bird, often mistaken for a bumblebee. This hummingbird's wings beat with the force of a turbo engine, but its heart can be broken with the pressure of a thumb. It is amazing that in this world of little things we are ruled by someone so big that we cannot help but feel small. As if we too have come to rest in another's palm.*

There are things I miss that I never thought I would. The sea is not the same because this one crashes against rocks and the earth is red and must be coaxed for something to grow. There is no scent of lemons, no sweet fruits I can pluck from the trees. These Spaniards wear black and are serious about life. I never wake to music blaring,

people dancing in the street. No one throws cowrie shells at the
ground to predict what lies ahead.

I miss the color of mangoes, fuchsia flowers. A hundred kinds of
palm trees, the dolphins that swam beside me in the sea. But some
places, like some people, are best loved from afar. Some places are
better when they are remembered.

Eight

THE DAY after Isabel stood me up, she left a message at the hotel. The desk clerk smiled as he handed me a slip of paper, torn from a child's notebook. I could barely decipher her penciled scrawl. She wrote that there had been a problem with the buses and she had been delayed, that there was no phone in the district where she was so she couldn't call. She pleaded with me to return, to come back and see her again.

The next afternoon I made my way through the same tangle of vines, the same maze of thorny bushes that I'd come down the day before. The untended fruit trees had dropped their rotten fruit. A rodent peered at me, then scurried away with a tamarind between his orange teeth as I knocked on the door, which was on the floor below where Rosalba lived. On the door of Isabel's apartment were two hand-painted pink hearts, with Isabel's and her daughter Milagro's names intertwined.

Milagro let me in. She was a large, sturdy girl of about

thirteen, as tall as her mother and almost twice her size, with gold baubles in her ears. A "Boss" Springsteen T-shirt clung to her burgeoning breasts. But she had her mother's deep black eyes, her thick black hair that fell around her shoulders. "Mummy's in here," she said.

The apartment smelled of incense and mint tea. Flower petals were strewn across the floor as if some secret ritual was being practiced here. The rooms with the shades wide open were as light as Rosalba's were dark, and the heat of the day poured in. Salsa spewed forth from the radio and a song called "Latin Lover" played. Milagro lip-synched the words as she led me into the middle of the sparsely furnished room, to a Formica table and a bouquet of plastic flowers.

Sunken on the couch missing its springs, Isabel sat, looking more like a child than her own daughter. Milagro touched her mother on the shoulder. "Mummy, here's your friend." Then Milagro raised her mother up as if she were helping an invalid.

"Oh, Milie," Isabel said, "I'm not that old. I'm only thirty-five."

Carved saints with pleading hands and despondent gazes lined the mantel. On the wall were pictures of Jesus, Marilyn Monroe, a Rosalba who looked like the Elizabeth Taylor of *la isla*, and Isabel with her daughter. Except for Jesus there were no pictures of men. There was none of her father, though there was a poster of a singing group, Hijos de Andalucía.

"Let's go somewhere else," Isabel whispered. She pointed to each of the four walls, making a circling motion with her hands. Milagro turned the volume up on the music, pressing her fingers to her lips. "It is best not to speak here," Isabel said.

I don't like whispering. I never have. When we were young, Lydia and I always spoke in hushed tones, afraid to be heard. "I don't want to hear a peep out of you girls," our father would say to us at night, "not a sound." He aimed his finger our way so we knew he meant it. At home we spoke with a hand cupped to ear or in codes, by semaphore. A finger pointing downstairs, a thumb motioning outside. Whenever we could, we walked in the woods around our house. But even there we never raised our voices. Lydia now tells me how she remembers darkness, drawn shades, rooms without light. But what I remember are whispers.

Isabel led me down long winding streets, through alleyways where children played with a discarded bicycle wheel and sticks. They rolled the wheel down muddy streets, garbage-strewn alleyways. There were no sandlot baseball games, no one shooting hoops. No bats, no balls.

The streets were riddled with potholes. Huge craters pitted the roads as if they'd been bombed, and the few cars twisted past them as if through a maze. We passed a building with the first floor gutted, but a family living on the second floor. On the balcony a hen strutted; laundry of tattered undershirts and blue jeans flapped in the breeze.

Along the Miramar, people wore cardboard signs, attached around their necks with string. At first I thought this was some form of public humiliation. But then I looked closer. A young couple with a small child wore a sign that said they wanted a two-bedroom anywhere in exchange for their one-bedroom in the center of the city. A single man who wished to marry was trying to convince an old woman who wanted to leave her large apartment that his studio was near the sea.

We walked for a long time and I was hot and tired. But

Isabel moved like a dancer, her arms reaching before her into space. Sweat beads formed on the corners of her brow, but other than that she moved effortlessly. I followed and we did not speak.

At last we arrived at a café not far from the sea and the old cemetery. We sat down and looked around, waiting to be served, but no waiter came. Though the café was open, no one was working there. My mouth was parched, but there was nothing to drink. "I'm so thirsty," I said. "Isn't there anything?" Isabel went into the back of the café and returned with two glasses of warm tap water.

I stared into my glass. "It's okay," Isabel said, "you can drink it. One of the few things my father has really done is make the water pure." Sipping slowly, we sat facing each other with a view of the sea. "I like to come here," Isabel said, "because my first husband is buried over there. My second husband as well." She pointed to the old cemetery, which wasn't far away. "I loved the first one and I liked the second one a lot. It's a long story."

I looked at her, surprised. "Oh, I go through men like I'd go through money if I had any." She laughed. "I've been married four times now. Milagro is the child of my third husband. My fourth was a businessman from Caracas. I married him to get me out of here, but of course my visa was denied. When I go to immigration, do you know what they say to me? They say I will never leave. They grin at me when they tell me this. They say that I will die here just like the rest of them."

Isabel took out a packet of cigarettes, Marlboros, in fact, tamped it, and offered me one.

"No, thanks," I shook my head. I hadn't had a cigarette in nine years.

Isabel shrugged, indifferent to my good or bad habits. She lit one, tilted her head back, and blew smoke into the sky as I sipped the water she'd brought me in slow, careful sips. As she held the cigarette between her fingers, I noticed for the first time her nails, which, like mine, were bitten down to the quick. "You're married?" she asked, pointing to my ring.

"Yes, and I have a daughter." I fumbled in my wallet, though the pictures I carried were a few years old.

"Oh, she is beautiful. She looks just like you," Isabel said, her face lightening for the first time.

I didn't want to argue that she doesn't look like me. "But she acts like her father," I said.

"And how is that?"

"Oh, she's chaotic; I'm more orderly."

"But she's just a child," Isabel said with a laugh. "Do you leave them often?"

I shook my head. "Not often, but it is good to get away. I find it gives me a new perspective."

"Yes, I imagine it does." She gave me a wry smile. "I wouldn't know."

"Oh, I'm sorry . . ."

"It's all right. In fact, I've never been anywhere. You know, when we toast in this country, we don't say 'salud;' we say 'visa.' We all want to leave, but there are no exit visas. My father is tyrant. What more can I say."

I wanted to ask about her father, but her bitterness surprised me and Isabel seemed agitated, almost angry. "It's hard to imagine. I've always been free . . ."

"Of course you have. How could you know, but it's all I want, you see. To get away." She sighed, gazing out to sea.

"And you can't . . ."

"Oh, no"—she laughed a nervous laugh—"he'll never let

me go." Isabel paused. "Believe me, I'm a prisoner, as surely as if I were behind bars."

As we sipped our water in a deserted café off the Miramar, Isabel told me that she had once lived in a house of many rooms that opened onto the sea. Its wide doors were never shut, except during the most violent storms; its windows let in the breeze. At night she was lulled to sleep by the surf pounding the shore, and every morning she awakened to the same sound, and it became the rhythm of her days and her nights. Even now, years after she moved into the ground-floor apartment, over a mile from the sea, she still thinks she wakes to the sound of the surf.

In the house where she grew up, there were yellow curtains in her room and yellow flowers in the vase. She had a yellow cat named Topaz who slept at the foot of her bed in the pools of golden sun that poured in. Fruit trees bloomed outside her window and some mornings Mercedes—the ancient nanny who had come to the family when she herself was not more than a child to care for Rosalba and had stayed with them all these years—plucked tamarind and papaya ripe from their branches. Each morning at seven Mercedes brought her a tray of warm milk and almond biscuits, a boiled egg, and fresh-squeezed juice while her parents ate alone downstairs.

The man who called himself her father was a small man with blue eyes whom her mother had married when she was just a girl. Umberto Calderón always wore a black suit and smelled of antiseptic soaps and lingering disease. He was a dermatologist who specialized in skin ailments of the tropics. But his patients were mainly the wealthy of *la isla* who wanted him to cure their age spots, the dark blotches and moles that blossomed in the relentless sun and made Dr.

Calderón's medical practice flourish almost as much as did the business of the island's only abortionist (whom the Calderón women would visit from time to time).

Isabel's older half sister, Serena, had her mother's and father's blue eyes and soft brown hair—the genetic vestiges of the Spanish aristocracy that once ruled. But Isabel had dark eyes and dark hair, and when she looked into the face of the man who called himself her father she knew that she was looking at a stranger. Umberto Calderón, also, had no doubt as to his daughter's parentage. He informed his beautiful wife, whom he adored, that as long as she did not humiliate him, he would accept the child, giving her his name, but never his heart.

One day a Portuguese freighter, filled with sailors, crashed into their seawall, and the sailors had to stay for a week until their ship was repaired and towed out to sea. During that time the sailors taught Isabel how to tie knots and do a dance in which she clapped her heels. They let her wear their hats and told her stories of monsters they'd seen rising out of the darkest seas.

When the sailors left, Isabel begged them to take her with them but they laughed and gave her a hat to keep. She wore it around the house for years.

She was miserable when Umberto came home from his trips to the outer ends of the island, where he tended the needs of wealthy *finca* owners and ladies who guarded over the sugarcane plantations that their fathers had purchased in Spain. He returned with gifts for Serena, but nothing for her. She missed the Portuguese sailors and held on to dreams of stowing away. She did not see why when there was an outing to the beach she would be left behind to wander the rooms of the big house with Mercedes in tow. And then one day she understood.

Mercedes got her up early and told her she had to dress in her prettiest clothes. Mercedes put bows in her hair and fluffed up her skirt. And then Mercedes took her downstairs. Her mother sat in the living room with a man who looked familiar to her, though she did not know from where. He was tall and his eyes were black and shiny as polished stones and he wore a soldier's uniform. "So," he said as Isabel was brought in, "this is the child." And for a moment Isabel thought that she was going to be taken away from everything she knew.

Rosalba said, "Come closer, Isabel, come here."

Tentatively Isabel walked toward him. She smelled his cigars, the rum, and she smelled her mother's perfume. He towered above her, more like a monument than a man, and she tilted her head back in order to get a better look, and this made him laugh. Perhaps there was a statue with his and other soldiers' faces on it at the Plaza of the Heroes of the Revolution (there was not). Or perhaps she had glimpsed him on television, pounding his fists during late-night harangues as her mother listened, spellbound.

But it wasn't in any of these places that Isabel had seen him before. Rather, she looked up and stared into his dark eyes and found her own. "She looks just like you," she heard her mother say.

The year when I turned eight, Isabel said, my real father came and danced with me. My mother and her husband, Umberto Calderón, whom I called Papi until the day he died, had gone to a conference in Spain, and in the evening when I was already in my nightgown in my bed, a large, dark car pulled up. A door slammed and I heard a low whistle. Without a word, Mercedes let him in.

He wore a suit of camouflage that looked like falling leaves. He said he'd come to dance with me. I had no idea what he meant, but he put a record on the phonograph. It was a marimba band, playing mambos, and he knew the steps very well. Step together one two three he showed me as he took me into his arms. "I want to see," he said, "if you can follow me." He pressed me to him and I felt his arms around my waist.

I was a little girl and he twirled me around the room like a mop, my feet sweeping the floor. All the arms that had ever held me were women's arms—pale, thin. But his were wide and strong. He hummed the music into my ears. He was a delicate dancer and I felt light as a plucked flower in his arms.

He smelled of ashes and rum, but I could see what it must have been like for my mother when she fell in love with him. Then he stopped dancing and told me he had to go away for a while and it might be a long time before he would see me again. "You are my little one," he told me. *Mi hijita.* "The world is changing. You'll see. Everything will change. You can join me. Your mother chose not to and that of course was her decision. But I will come back for you and together we will make the world a different place."

When he left, he touched Mercedes on the arm and I knew she had agreed to let him come. He patted me on the head and said, "Don't tell your mother I was here tonight. It is our secret."

I never told my mother. After he went away, I wrote him a letter, which Mercedes promised to mail for me. "When the moon is high, I think you will come and dance with me again. I listen for your whistle, but it is always the wind. The other day there was a fire and a dog was burned alive. I can still hear him howling. I hope you will come back soon."

But he never answered my letter. He never came back to dance with me again. I would see him from time to time at official functions and he'd come over and touch me on the head. Sometimes, when Umberto was away, he came to our house and I could hear his voice rumbling in another room. But it would be many years before he tried to see me again. And then only by sending his lawyers to come and claim me.

Not long after his visit, when she was still waiting for his return, Isabel woke and felt a weight on her chest. The room was dark and she could not see, but something heavy lay there. Mercedes told her once that if she ever woke and found a snake in her bed, not to move or breathe. That it was only looking for a warm place to sleep. In the morning it would wake and slither outside again, returning the way it had come.

For the rest of that night Isabel lay on her back, with the snake on her chest, trying not to breathe. She did not know what kind of snake it was but she knew that the Caribe rattler, brought from Africa on slave ships, lived in the moist, sandy woods not far from the house. For hours she lay perfectly still, her breath shallow, afraid the snake would feel the rise and fall of her chest.

In the morning as first light entered the room, Mercedes came in to wake Isabel and she found the girl, immobile, staring at the ceiling with a snake coiled on her chest. Isabel only blinked as Mercedes stopped, cupping her hand over her mouth, then raced out of the room. She returned with a campesino who clutched a machete in his fist, and he nudged the snake. Isabel watched as the snake unwound itself, raising its head and writhing on her chest. She heard it rattle.

As the snake hissed and prepared to strike, the man swooshed the blade through the air above Isabel's chest and sliced off the snake's head in one clean stroke.

For hours after that, though her sheets were covered in blood, neither Mercedes nor Rosalba could get Isabel to move. She had no idea how long she remained frozen there, breathing her shallow breaths.

"You see," Isabel told me, "it's as if I can still feel that snake on my chest. And I'm waiting for the morning when it will go away."

Nine

IN THE LOBBY of the hotel I have noticed a smell. The
smell of bodies. This is because there is no soap in *la isla*;
the people cannot bathe. There is water—cold water—but
they have no soap. When the waiters bring me my coffee in
the morning, I tip them with bars of soap.

I am sitting at the little table I have staked out for myself. It
has become my place. It helps under these conditions to
establish routines, create familiar things. My table, my room,
my waiter, my shower curtain, my Major Lorenzo. I am trying to read the newspaper, but it is difficult to concentrate
because of the sound of breaking balls.

A pool game is going on in earnest in the corner. I listen
to the clacking of balls, the groans of players as they miss their
shots. I get up and chalk a cue. "Rack them up," I say to the
group of Dutch boys. One of the blond men smirks as he
puts the balls in the triangle, but one of the few things I
know how to do in this world is play pool. My father had me
racking balls on our basement pool table when I could barely

see over the rail. I notice that two balls are missing. "You break," I tell him. And he smashes the cue ball toward the center of the triangle. The ball makes odd, sliding movements along the green felt, which is torn, and the slate beneath it is not lying flat.

The table is old, circa 1950s. My guess is that someone dug it up out of a storage room in one of the casinos, where it had been sitting in dampness for the past thirty years. The Dutchman's break sinks one ball, then he scratches. It is my shot and I line up a combination, put a little English on, and watch the cue ball wobble across the table. No one is sure where anything will go, but the five ball sinks into the side pocket. Though I'd been aiming for the seven in the corner, everyone applauds.

"Nice shot," a young woman says. She is wearing a short red dress and has pretty dark hair. "Don't I know you from somewhere?" she asks me. I know that I've seen her before too. I finish my game, though it is all hit-or-miss. I sink a few balls, but lose. When I return to where I had been sitting, the woman in the red dress is sitting there.

"*¿La molesto?*" she asks me. "All the tables are filled."

"No problem," I tell her, "please join me," though I notice that the tables aren't filled.

"My friends are here too," she says, pointing to my extra chairs.

"Them too," I say.

Her friends also have short skirts, thick makeup on. They wear giant gold earrings, the size of door knockers. One wears a pink and black spotted jumpsuit. There aren't many women with the body for this kind of a jumpsuit, but this woman has one. They introduce themselves. Their names are María, Eva, and Flora and they remind me of the three birds on my dentist's drill when I was a girl. Which birdie is singing? Dr. Yeagar used to ask as he drilled.

"I'm sure I've seen you before," María, the woman in the red dress, says.

"Probably just from the other day," I reply.

"No," she says, shaking her head, "it was a long time ago."

"So," says Eva, who has red lipstick and wears a short skirt, "you just get here?" Suddenly I recognize her as the woman who was with one of the Finnish men. María, who is smiling, was with the dwarf. "Yes, just yesterday."

"Oh, where you from?" María asks. "Canada?"

"No, America, actually."

"America? This is America," says Flora, in the black and pink spandex.

"The United States," I reply.

Distracted, Flora, who is black, looks away. "Oh that one."

"So perhaps you have things you'd like to sell? Underwear? Blue jeans?" Eva plucks at my jeans.

"I just have soap." I hand them a few bars, which I keep in my bag. They hold them and sniff. "You can keep these," I say, and for the moment they seem content. Flora tucks hers between her breasts. Suddenly there is a flurry of activity. A tour group from Germany has just arrived and María, Eva, and Flora stand up to excuse themselves. "Duty calls," María says, giving me a wave of her hand, containing a bar of apricot soap. Her hips move as she heads to the counter, where a tired German traveler is just checking in.

Major Lorenzo crosses her path, but his eyes do not settle on her at all. Instead he scans the room, and when he spots me he waves. As he approaches with his aide trailing behind him, the staff and guests all look my way. Enrique cannot miss this; neither can the prostitutes as they now move toward the bar. I receive significant stares, then everyone turns away.

"So," he says, "how are you? Have you found everything you need?"

His asking is a formality but I assure him that everything is fine. Pulling back an extra chair, I invite Major Lorenzo to join me for drink, but with a wave of his hand he refuses. He does not say it, but, of course, this could be misinterpreted; it could be perceived as a bribe.

"At least sit with me," I say, because I feel comfortable at this table.

"No," he says, his voice firm. "I prefer to wait for you in the lobby."

When I finish my coffee, I join him. He rises as he sees me coming, extending his hand. He wants to know if everything is all right. If there is anything he can do to make my stay more comfortable. I am certain that under other circumstances he would invite me out for coffee, perhaps to his house to meet his wife. He is trim and fit and tells me he bicycles each day. Not because he has to, he assures me, not because he cannot get gasoline for his car, but because he wants to stay fit. He pounds his chest and it is tight as a drum.

The two men who accompany him are also fit, but they are much younger so it is less impressive. They are also more frightening behind their reflector shades with guns strapped to their hips. Major Lorenzo doesn't wear a weapon. He doesn't wear reflector shades. "So," he says, "we are trying to move forward. To get you back as soon as we can."

"Yes, I suppose that would be best."

"There are, however, some delays. Technicalities that hopefully we will clear up soon." I ponder pressing him, asking him once again for the reason I am here. Yet I think it is better if I don't push him. He has been so considerate of my needs, providing me with a room with a view. He does not wish to disturb my coffee. He has been so kind, really, and yet I have this sense that I would not want to cross him, that it might not be the right thing to do.

"So," he says, "have you spoken with your daughter?" His daughter is sixteen, he tells me, and she wants to be a veterinarian when she grows up. "Do you have a picture?" he asks. Fumbling in our wallets, we produce pictures of our children, both apologizing that the photos are old. His daughter has crooked teeth, which Major Lorenzo says already have braces and that she is taller than he. Then he gazes at my snapshot of Jessica. Like Isabel, he says that she looks just like me, which isn't true so I know that he is being polite. And this makes me wonder if there isn't something that he too wants from me. A confession or the whereabouts of the disappeared. But the truth is, and perhaps Isabel has seen to this, I have no idea what happened to her. I have no idea where she is.

Though it is only five o'clock in the afternoon, I find I am suddenly tired after he leaves. There is nothing really that I want to do, and I seem to have no energy for anything anyway. It is as if I have somehow been drained of my strength. I go up to my room, thinking I'll lie down for a moment. My head rests on the soft pillow. My hands grope at the cool sheets. The room is darkened, the French doors closed. Outside there are shouts, laughter.

I do not remember falling asleep, but soon I am dreaming. I am in a jungle where howler monkeys shake the branches overhead. Blue morpho butterflies loom. A capybara lumbers through the woods. Suddenly the sky darkens and turns a winter's gray. At first only a light snow falls, but then it gets heavier, thick and billowy.

I grow smaller, more compact. I'm in a snowsuit, heading into the jungle where now the snow falls densely. The jungle becomes a forest. My hands wear mittens, a scratchy scarf covers my face. I find a trail of human tracks and I follow these through the snow.

Ten

ONCE WHEN I was a girl, there was an ice storm, and for days we couldn't go to school or drive to the store. We skated up and down the street, but mostly Lydia and I stayed inside, where we played games. We pretended our beds were continents, the floor a roiling sea. For hours we jumped from bed to bed, never touching the floor, where we'd drown.

We played trading places, though we didn't look anything alike. Everything about her was long, even her fingers and her nose; even though I am older, I am small, round, and brown, like an acorn. But for a day I was Lydia and she was me. We put on each other's clothes. Hers were too big and I had to roll them up, and her ankles showed when she wore my pants, as if she had just outgrown them.

We switched beds. I did her English homework and she did my math. She could do math fractions in her head while I wrote an essay on why I liked to ice skate (which is what she liked to do). She liked to get out on the ice and twirl, and she never fell because she had strong ankles, but I tripped over my feet, bruised my bottom on the ice. Still, I wrote how I loved to feel my feet beneath me as they glided, how I loved hot chocolate and rosy cheeks, when in fact I've always been someone who loves warm, open places, surf pounding the shore.

I called her friends and made dates and she called mine. When our father hollered for Lydia to come downstairs and set the table, I came. He got so angry it was almost funny to see, the way his face wrinkled up and his eyes set their sights on me as if he'd hit me, but he never did. Instead he shouted, I didn't call you, I called Lydia.

I told him, Daddy, I'm Lydia today, but he didn't think that was funny. He didn't find it funny at all.

My father didn't like to be in the house, which our mother had furnished from a Sears catalog. He wanted to be at the office or in his "studio," which was the unheated garage. He ran a small manufacturing firm, before it went bankrupt, that made plastic ashtrays, ice packs, and plastic handles for hamburger presses. The ashtrays had three designs in them that he'd drawn himself—horses, dogs, antique cars. Perfect for the sporty set, he'd joke. He had schemes for other things he wanted to do—refrigerator magnets, party balloons.

In the garage during the warmer months our father painted. He painted mostly seascapes, landscapes, and cities from postcards—usually Paris in the rain. Lydia and I would go out there in the summer and he'd give us a brush and some paint and we'd try to copy his paintings on pieces of paper he'd tack to the trees. Whenever Lydia asked him to paint us, he always said, "I don't do people."

When it was cold, he tried to paint in the basement, but he

complained that we bothered him too much. "There's not enough room here," he'd say to our mother of the two-bedroom ranch house they'd never pay off.

The January of the ice storm, there was a thaw and the thaw brought rain. It rained and rained, and as the temperature fell the rain glazed the trees, the power lines, the roads. Lydia and I saw fairy castles in the glass and pretended to be snow queens while our father tried to break up the ice in the driveway with a pickax, whacking like a prisoner trying to escape. But the driveway was too long and the ice too thick, and once he had broken it up there was nowhere to go.

We dressed up in long cotton skirts and our mother made grilled cheese sandwiches. We ate them in front of the fireplace with pickles and potato chips. The sandwiches were hot with thick, runny cheese, and the pickles stung my tongue. When we were done, our father said to carry our dishes back to the kitchen. Lydia never wanted to carry heavy things because she dropped them, so I loaded up the tray. But when I passed our father on the three stairs that connected the living room to the kitchen, he said, "Maggie, you're going to drop that tray."

"I won't," I told him.

His nostrils flared; his jaw was set firm. "Yes, you will." Even as he said it, I felt my foot tangling in my skirt. The tray grew heavy in my hands, tilting as the dishes slipped forward. I listened as the dishes tumbled down the stairs, shattering on the floor. "You see," my father said, as he walked away, "I told you you would."

Eleven

THE RINGING of the phone wakes me and for a moment I am not sure where I am. My surroundings aren't familiar and I cannot recall what city I am in or how I got here. Then I hear a voice, speaking Spanish to me. "I'm afraid I've woken you," the voice says apologetically, and I know it is Major Lorenzo. I struggle to sit up.

"It's all right. I should be getting up." I reach for my watch, which is on the nightstand, and see that it is only eight o'clock in the morning, but I have been asleep since the previous afternoon. There is a hollow pit in my stomach and suddenly I am very hungry.

"There are some people who would like to see you."

"Oh," I say, "are they here?"

"No," he replies, drawing out the word, as if this thought never would have occurred to him, "we are going there."

"I'll be down in a few minutes," I tell him. I am about to get up, to shower quickly, but as I lie there, I am struck with the odd feeling that I have not been alone, as if someone has been in the room, watching me. Looking at my belongings, at me as I slept. I am warm, sweating, as I get up and go through my things. My head seems to be reeling, as if I have fallen into a dead sleep. I open drawers, peer into the closet. Scan the walls for holes, hidden cameras. Everything seems to be in place, as I left it. When I close my eyes, I can almost hear another person breathing, yet I know no one is there. Still I undress in the bathroom, where I take a cold shower; I put on my clothes before leaving the bathroom.

That is when I notice the frog. It is a small, green frog, wedged between the wall of the bathroom and a window that must have once opened onto the outside. How the frog got into my room, let alone into that wedged place between the window and the wall, I'll never know. But it makes a deep, guttural sound. The window is locked shut, so I'll try to find a maid to let the frog out.

As I leave the room, I see a maid and signal to her, but she just looks at me, then scurries away. I hear her whispering to another worker in the corridor as I walk by. They know, I tell myself. Everyone knows who I am. And what I have done.

Major Lorenzo sits in the lobby, leaning forward, speaking with his aide, who even inside wears his reflector shades. I have yet to see his eyes. Major Lorenzo is dressed in perfect military attire and looks like a man who is going somewhere. As soon as he sees me, he stops talking and rises. So does his aide, and people turn, looking my way, since there aren't many men around in reflector shades with semiautomatic weapons strapped to their waists.

Major Lorenzo extends his hand and I notice that he smells of after shave. Canoe? Old Spice? Some brand my father used to wear. "Well, Maggie," Major Lorenzo says, calling me by my first name for the first time, "I'm sorry we disturbed you." He motions for me to sit down.

"It's all right," I tell him, "I have things to do."

Both men give me quizzical looks, wondering what that could possibly be. I shrug, pointing to my nails. "A manicure," I say, and they laugh. Major Lorenzo has coffee and toast waiting for me and he sits beside me impassively as I gobble it down.

Stepping out into the plaza, I am blinded by the light and the heat of the day. In the short time I have been here, I find I am growing accustomed to drawn shades, the subdued light filtered through them. Major Lorenzo holds my elbow as I step down from the curb, as if we are on a date. Perhaps now we will go out for coffee, have lunch at El Colibrí. I feel the sturdy cobblestones beneath my feet. Solid ground.

People saunter past—full-bodied women move in languorous steps as if they have just risen from their beds. Men strut; others mill about, smoking cigars. Suddenly I am gripped with the urge to run, to dash away, to lose myself in the throngs. I've seen this in my dog. Sometimes he gets out and races down the street and I know that what he wants to do, what it is in his heart to do, is to run away.

But I do not break free. I do as I am told. Major Lorenzo opens the door to the plain beige car I traveled in before. His aide waits until I am comfortably seated inside. Then the two of them sit in front, Major Lorenzo with his arm draped over the back of the seat, turning to me from time to time. "Is it too much air?" he asks as he did when he first brought me here. "Did you have enough to eat?" I am torn between feeling like a visiting dignitary and a truant child en route to some official reprimand, my disgruntled parents in the front seat.

We drive inland, away from the sea, and this disappoints me, since I was hoping we would follow the water. I want to take deep breaths. Instead the air grows heavy and thick. We move swiftly down the winding roads that lead away from Puerto Angélico, twisting so many times that I am not sure whether we are going to the east or the west.

I have always had a good sense of direction, but now I cannot seem to get my bearings. I try to find markers so I'll remember the way—a billboard, a sports arena, a road sign, but everything seems generic, nondescript, though I know I have never taken this road before. Isabel never brought me this way, so there cannot be much of interest here.

Bloodred mariposa and wandering primrose cling to the median strip, but along the sides of the road the vegetation is thick, junglelike. Once again there is that sticky-sweet smell of overripe fruit. Palmettos, banana trees arch across the road. Perhaps there is a rain forest they want me to see. Something for the ecotourist market. A secret jungle joint-venture hotel, an inland lake resort about to be opened. Or perhaps there is an important person who wants to meet me. I think of all the houses of El Caballo—the hunting lodge, the *finca*. He thinks I have information to share with him. I will tell him what little I know and they will let me go home. I picture a veranda by a pool, a cold luncheon plate of shrimp and little crabs from the sea.

We become trapped behind the back of a bus. Diesel fumes spew into the car and Major Lorenzo grows impatient. He tells the driver to lean on his horn, to drive up on the sidewalk. He must not want to keep whomever it is waiting.

For the first time the aide puts on our siren and the bus pulls over to the side of the road so we can speed by.

Soon the vegetation drops back, the road widens, and we turn off onto a dirt road lined with cinder-block buildings, institutional structures that sit on dry, burned-out fields, and this does not appear to be where the head of a small island nation would live. It doesn't even seem to be where he would work. And then I see the barbed wire around the buildings, the bars on the windows. These are prisons, and I know because I have written about this in my guidebook—that they are full.

It occurs to me what has not exactly occurred before. That anything could happen. That they could lock me up and lose the key. "Where are we going?" I ask Major Lorenzo, my voice trembling.

"Oh, it is here. It will be all right. The head of immigration just wants to ask you a few questions."

We pass buildings in disrepair, crumbling. Others appear to be abandoned. This does not seem like the place where the head of immigration would have his offices. We park in front of one of the cinder-block buildings, surrounded with razor wire. "Looks just like my neighborhood," I say with a nervous laugh, thinking of the city where I live, but they don't get the joke. At least, they don't seem to.

Major Lorenzo looks at me without expression, as if I am not really there, as if he can see through me. I want him to tell me where we really are and what I can expect, but he looks away. "We'll get out now," he says. His aide leaps from the car and opens my door, then they usher me quickly inside.

The building has a doorway with no door and windows with no glass. No lights are on inside. It is stifling as a cave when we go in and I am struck by the odor of bodies, a thick smell like what I imagine a men's locker room would have. In the foyer a man in uniform sits at a desk, nodding when Major Lorenzo enters. With a turn of his head, he motions us to one side, where there are two chairs.

"Maggie," Major Lorenzo says, touching my arm for the second time, "why don't you sit there?"

It is hot and I almost collapse onto the folding chair. We wait for what seems like a long time. Several minutes, in fact. I fan myself with a newspaper I find lying on the floor and Major Lorenzo fans himself with his hat. "Would you like something cold to drink?" he asks.

"Yes, that would be very nice." Is this the way you really are? I want to ask him. At night alone with your wife and kid? Do you bring them ice water? Do you take your wife's arm as she steps off a curb? Or is it just for people under house arrest? As he asks for a glass of water from one of the soldiers standing around, I think to myself that I like him. I can't help it. I don't want anything to come between us. I allow my arm to rest against his. I feel the sensation of cloth against cloth, and he does not pull his arm away.

Before the glass of water arrives, a door opens and another man in uniform motions for us to come into the room. This room is windowless with a large metal desk in the middle. The calendar on the wall hasn't been changed in the past three months, which depresses me more than anything else. Several folding chairs are against the wall and Major Lorenzo and the man who opened the door for us take seats there. They motion for me to take the folding chair in front of the desk.

I almost expect to see the colonel with the dead eyes from the airport sitting at the desk. Instead I find myself facing an overweight man with greasy skin. His blue guayabera is mottled with sweat; wet circles are under his arms. "We'd just like to ask you a few questions," the overweight man says. With his round face and small mustache, he reminds me of John Wayne Gacy, the murderer of boys who dressed like a clown. "You speak Spanish very well, I understand. Where did you learn?"

"In the street," I say, then realize this may not be the right response. "In Mexico. I've traveled around."

"Well, we just want to know something about your activities, about what you are doing here."

"Yes, of course."

There is a door behind him and it opens. I expect to hear the cries of torture, anguished pleas. Someone begging for mercy. Instead a coffee pot and cups are produced on a tray. So this is to be a social visit, after all. A soldier walks around, pouring. Major Lorenzo takes his with sugar. I ask for mine with milk. He obliges us. This is very civilized, I tell myself, for an interrogation.

"We'd like to know what you are doing here," the overweight man says. "Who are you working for?"

I take a sip of my coffee, but immediately feel hot and shaky. I wish I hadn't worn a dress, because already I feel my thighs sticking to the chair. "I'm working for a travel-guide company, Easy Rider Guides. I go to countries and revise the guidebooks. That is what I do. You can call my boss and ask him." He smirks at this, as does the man in uniform sitting next to Major Lorenzo. These are men who are accustomed to having their security violated, their meetings infiltrated. Disinformation is nothing new to them.

"Yes, but you have been here before, haven't you?" the overweight man says. Leaning forward, I notice that he has a thick file in front of him. Somewhere in the building a door slams, and I jump slightly in my chair. Everyone puts their cups of coffee down. "What was the purpose of your visit that time?"

"It was for my work. I was updating our Caribbean travel guide."

He nods, leaning his arms on the thick file. "And that's all."

"Yes, that's all."

"Did you meet any people while you were on *la isla*?"

Now my whole body is suddenly warm, my skin prickly. Sweat breaks out under my arms, between my breasts. I long for something cold to drink, but what would they bring me? Orange Fanta, tap water. "I met a few people, the way you do when you are traveling."

"Yes, of course. And do you remember who any of those people were?"

There is a rustling in the room as this question is asked. I hear legs shifting, sighs. I am trembling as he asks this because I have never been very good at lying, but now I must look him in the eye and do just that. "Not really, I don't remember anyone in particular. You know, I was working very hard . . ." The room is stifling now and I find myself growing dizzy, weak. Though I have never fainted before, I wonder if I am going to now.

The overweight man lights up a cigarette and begins to smoke. "Of course, Miss Conover, we know that you work very hard. And, of course, it is in our interest that you see our country in the best possible light. But some people would have you see us differently. Now please try again. We are not in a hurry. In fact, we have plenty of time."

The room is quiet, as if there is no one else in here except me and this fat man. Now he shuffles his papers, packs them like a deck of cards. Then he leans forward, smiling slightly at me. "Now why don't you try harder. If you'd like, you could have some time alone." He takes a drag, then puts out his cigarette. He looks back at me but he is not smiling now. "There must be someone you remember."

Twelve

THERE IS A ROAD that twists along the sea on the south side of the island that leads from Puerto Angélico to some of the most beautiful, remote beaches of the world. But almost no one goes there because they are so far from the National Highway that cuts straight across the island, dividing it in two. There are no gas stations along this road, so unless you carry extra gasoline you'll run out of fuel. Isabel didn't seem to mind. She'd brought a pair of blue jeans and some Spam. "We'll barter for gas as we go," she said.

She drove her blue Chevy, circa 1955, full speed ahead. The car was a mass of handmade spare parts held together with chicken wire. The battery connection was made with the head of a coat hanger, and the floor was plasterboard. The bodywork had been done with poster paint. The windows were permanently rolled down. But it drove.

As she had instructed me, I'd brought a basket of cheese, crackers, peanut butter, and olives from the tourist *tienda*— none of which Isabel could get with her ration card. One chicken and a dozen eggs a month, a quart of milk a week. The jeans and Spam came from the black market. "I don't know how we survive," she told me.

We zoomed along the highway devoid of cars, lined with orange groves, mango trees. Her car made sputtering noises and sometimes she talked to it. "Come on, baby," she said, "don't break down." Fruit trees were everywhere. Cane fields burned. Dark swirls of smoke, like oncoming storms, rose. We cut off the main highway and headed toward the sea. Hitchhikers lined the roads, but Isabel shook her head. "Too many people know me," she said. "It's better not to stop." I watched an old woman with a milk pail try to flag us down.

She was taking me to Playa Negrita. Little Black Beach. The place of her father's biggest victory, of his enemy's biggest defeat. I was just a little girl, she said, but I remember how all the people danced in the street.

"Everyone who comes to *la isla*," Isabel said, "wants to know about my father. People who come here to see me— journalists, writers—all want to know about him. But I cannot talk about my father because I don't know him. I never saw him. When he came to the house, he patted me on the head, but after I was eight and he came to dance with me, he didn't come any more."

The man I called my father, Isabel said, who was my mother's husband, could never look me in the eye. He had a way of casting his gaze so that it was just around me or over me. But he never looked at me. If I crawled into his lap, he had a way of slipping out from under me. I could watch Serena stay in his lap, laughing, telling him stories, but the minute I came near, he had a patient coming. He heard footsteps at the door.

It was like my body smelled. Like I had the plague. I remember once Mercedes took me to church and we knelt and prayed for the poor lepers and afterward I asked her what the poor lepers were and she said people whose bodies are rotting. For weeks I searched my body for sores. If I came near him, he'd sneak out of the room. I asked my mother once why he did that and she said, "You can't do anything about it. It's just the way he is." But, of course, I adored him. It was just my luck to adore someone who was always trying to get away from me.

Now she turned off the main road onto a dirt road surrounded by dense vegetation. Mosquitoes suddenly filled the car and we swatted them away. "Is he still this way with you?" I asked as I scratched at my arms, watching them turn red.

"Oh, no. He died. Anyway, he left the country when I was still a girl. He took Serena with him. So after that, it was just my mother and me, but my mother, well, I hardly saw her. She loved the man and she loved the revolution. For her the two things were one."

I felt uncomfortable, asking her about this, but, like her mother, Isabel seemed to want to talk. In fact, it seemed as if she had to talk. "And your real father, the one they call El Caballo? You never saw him, he never came to you again?"

"Oh, he greeted me at the official functions my mother dragged me to. I used to stand in front of the television, listening to his speeches. Really that was the closest I got. I was just another person in the crowd, until I became an embarrassment."

"An embarrassment?"

"Oh, yes. I did things. I talked to people I shouldn't have talked to." I must have looked at her askance. "Oh, I don't mean people like you. I talked to the press. I gave interviews. I told the world what I really thought about this country and the way he runs it." She wrinkled her brow as if she had to catch herself from what she was saying, but I heard that bitterness come creeping back into her voice. She sighed and grew silent as the car dug into a deep pothole, bouncing out again. "This must seem strange to you. You probably come from a normal family. You send cards to one another; you visit for the holidays. Your mother cooks a turkey."

"I think I understand what you're talking about," I told her.

"Do you really think you can?"

I thought about this for a moment. "Yes, I think I can."

When I turned fourteen, Isabel went on, my father came to claim me as his own. I had only seen him a few times over the years, when he came to see my mother. Once or twice he held me by the shoulders and said that I'd grown. He never mentioned the letter I wrote him or the night he came to dance with me. Now he sent a team of lawyers to the house and they demanded to see me.

My mother began to scream, thinking they had come to take me away. No, they explained, I was being adopted. You see, my father himself was the offspring of an illicit union, his father having impregnated a fourteen-year-old girl who was the family maid. In the end she bore the old man six children, but he never married her. So now my father had come to save me from his illegitimate fate.

I hovered in a corner in a pink dress, listening as a white-haired lawyer with a red poppy in his lapel read a letter from my father, stating that he intended to legitimize my birth and acknowledge his paternity. He had made arrangements to nullify the paternity of Umberto Calderón, who had divorced my mother a few years before and was living with Serena in southern Florida. The lawyer wept as he read my father's letter. I felt like a bride whose hand was being asked for.

I had not seen my father in six years, since the night he had come to dance with me. My mother looked at me, pleading, as I told the lawyer that I was happy to accept my father's offer. But I had two requests: I would like my father to pick out a gift to commemorate this occasion and I would like him to deliver it himself.

The lawyer stared, confused, unsure of how to respond. What gift would you like? he asked.

He can decide, I told the lawyer. He could bring me a silver cat with marble eyes or a bird in a gilded cage or a German bicycle or a stereo so I can play my rock and roll; he can send me a dress made out of Chinese silk or a small painting of the sea. Whatever he wants to give me would be fine; but he must bring it himself.

The poor man looked at me horrified because he knew he could never deliver such a request. Nobody tells El Jefe what to do. Nobody expects him to do that.

Or you can tell him that he is a *pendejo* and he can go fuck himself. Tell my father if he wanted to adopt me, he should have thought of that years ago.

We arrived at a truly black beach, the volcanic sand as dark as night, the water a brilliant turquoise blue that blinded me. The sky seemed to melt into the sea. In a burst of fuchsia and lemon, ice plant carpeted the porous lava rock that rose from the shore. The air smelled of jasmine and the sea. A beautiful place for an invasion, Isabel said. Once there were red-footed birds and others shaped like scissors that dive-bombed straight into the sea. "Now," she said with a shrug, "they have gone."

She parked the car on the sand. Before I knew it, she had stripped down to a thin, black bikini, pulling off her sundress, flinging off her shoes. She left her clothes in a heap, then dashed straight for the water, her small feet kicking up sand. She plunged into the crystalline waters and disappeared beneath the waves.

A moment later I followed, perhaps less daringly, but I tossed my skirt and T-shirt into a pile and raced into the sea after her. The water was surprisingly warm and the salt stung my dry, wintry skin.

We dove in and out of the gentle, rolling waves, our bodies buoyant as we floated in the surf. We splashed and chased each other along the shore. She dove to my right, then to my left. She vanished behind me, then came up in front. Her legs tangled with mine and she pulled me down. In the water we struggled together, a knot of arms and legs. Then Isabel came up laughing and swam away.

She swam to a rim of the bay where the sea had carved a cave out of the rising rock. The cave was deep and cone-shaped, like a breast, and water lapped in the darkness against the far wall. Inside its darkness the water shimmered a blue-green; yellow and red fish darted through the water and it was like swimming in an aquarium. Isabel touched me on the arm. "A giant sea turtle lives somewhere in this cave." Then she dove with her eyes open into the clear sea. I swam beside her, following a spotted eel, then floated on my back.

I closed my eyes and may have even slept in the warm, dark cave, but then Isabel tapped me on the shoulder. "We shouldn't stay too long. The tide can catch us. People have drowned here." Last year, she told me, a young couple, making love in the water, was trapped by the rising tide; their bodies were found, joined and crushed, on a ridge in the back of the cave.

Slowly we swam back to the center of the bay, where our things lay, and Isabel flopped down beside me, her body wet and salty from the sea. She put on a big, wide-rimmed straw hat, tipping it carefully so that her face was shadowed from the sun, then slathered sunscreen all over herself. Pulling over the picnic basket, she took out oranges, a hunk of cheese. She bit into an orange, pulling back the skin. Then she peeled it, handing half to me.

Next she undid her halter and lay on her back, her small, dark breasts pointing upward to the sun. Breathing heavily, she let the sun beat down on her breasts and her face. She had been so pale when I met her, but she was turning brown. Sucking on my orange, I looked away.

Then she rolled over, and rested her chin on her hands. She smelled of suntan lotion and the zest of oranges. Her nipples dipped into the sand. "My parents—not Dr. Calderón, but my real father and mother—used to come to this beach," she said. "Not with me, they never brought me, but she told me they came here. Once, to prove what it looked like, my father brought me a jar of black sand. He called me Negrita, I suppose after the battle of Playa Negrita, which was the only one he had decisively won. And because I was a dark one like this beach. Sometimes they came back with fish, because he also liked to fish here. But mainly they went to get away because no one knew about Playa Negrita for years. I still have that little jar of black sand. It is the only gift he ever gave me.

"My mother would pack them a picnic—bread, cheese, wine, some fruit—and she'd pat me on the head as I watched them leave. I'd stand at the window, my face pressed to the glass. My mother would come back late in the evening, her face burned, flecks of black sand in her hair that sparkled like the night sky. When she bathed afterward, the tub would be lined with this fine, black sand. Then she would move around the house in her nightgown, distracted and miserable, for days. I have never seen anything like it before or since." Isabel paused, rubbing cream into her legs. "But my mother was in love. It was as simple as that."

Now she looked at me, stared at me hard. "Have you ever been in love?" That look of sadness I had first noticed at the hotel came over her face, the kind that has no bottom.

"Yes, I have. Of course I have . . ." I loved Todd, but I wondered if that was the proper answer to her question.

"Well, I have. I didn't understand when I was a girl. But I understand now. I lost everything." I reached across and touched her hand. "You can't imagine what it is like for me. I have no work; I have nothing I can do. Except for my daughter, I have no one. I am always being followed. Even as we sit here, I feel as if they are watching me."

Tears came to her eyes and I kept my hand on hers. "Isn't there something you can do? Can't someone help you?"

"No." She shook her head. Here on this beautiful beach she looked pathetic. "There really isn't anything. Even my own mother says there is nothing to be done."

"But there must be something . . ."

Shaking her head, she smiled at me with the wry smile I'd seen so many times now. As if to tell me that I do not know anything. That I am naive and could not possibly understand.

She seemed to find me mildly amusing. Then she tapped me on the arm. "Come on," she said, rising, "let's swim."

I felt tired, lethargic in the sun and the heat and dispirited from her story, as if she had let some of that sadness out and I wasn't sure I wanted to know any more about it. "I'll follow you," I said, thinking I would take a nap.

She raced, diving into the waves. Then her head appeared like a cork, bobbing several yards out to sea, beyond the breakers. She swam in smooth, even strokes, perpendicular to the shore, and I was surprised at what a good swimmer she was. Gray clouds were mounting on the horizon, making long shadows across the water. A breeze picked up and there was a chill. It was as if darkness had descended all at once and I could barely make her out anymore.

Then I saw the fin. It was gray like the clouds and cut a path through the water, not moving swiftly, but slowly, the way the day had been, and it was heading straight for Isabel. I began to wave, to cup my hands and yell from the shore.

I jumped to my feet, rushed to the water's edge, shouting for her to turn around, but she continued her swim out and the big gray fish swam straight toward her. I was screaming madly now, racing into the waves, my feet burning on the sharp bits of coral beneath them. I pounded the water, thinking perhaps if I made a big disturbance the fish would be distracted and swim toward me. Instead it rose in a smooth arch and the sound of its splashing drowned out my voice so that even I could not hear it.

It seemed as if the fish were coming in for a strike, but then Isabel rose and descended and the fish rose again right after her. He was big and gray and they leaped together, then came down hard. When they did this again, rising up and coming down hard, I saw that they were playing, and that the fish was a dolphin, not a shark. I stood in knee-deep water, feeling somewhat stupid and thinking I should go in and join them. But it almost seemed as if this were a prearranged meeting. Something they'd planned. A rendezvous for just the two of them, and I could only stand on the shore and watch.

When Isabel came out of the water, she was flushed and smiling as I had not seen her smile before. She shook water over me like a dog. "I don't know what it is," she said, reaching for a towel, "but they always come to me."

Thirteen

WE ARE TRYING to move forward with your case," Major Lorenzo tells me as we speed back to the hotel, "but there are still some technicalities. The process is taking longer than we had imagined." It is midafternoon and I am tired. I also have not eaten and think that perhaps they have not either because they also look tired. Though Major Lorenzo did leave the room once while I was being questioned and was gone for quite a while, I don't think he went to have lunch. On the sides of their faces I can see their afternoon shadows starting to grow.

As Major Lorenzo speaks, I cannot see his face, only the movements of his jaw, because he is sitting with his back to me, staring straight ahead. My heart is beating faster. Why would this be taking longer? What could be wrong? "Well," I say, "can't we clear this matter up? I am anxious to get home . . ."

Now Major Lorenzo glances back at me, his face darkened. "Of course you are, but we don't think the matter will be cleared up so easily now, so soon . . ." He fumbles for words. "You should have been more forthcoming," he says hesitantly. "You should have told him what he wanted to know." I am silent when he says this, and it is as if we are both keeping a big secret and we can't even say it to each other. "You will probably have to stay in the hotel until we resolve what needs to be resolved."

"Yes, of course, I understand." Though I am not sure what needs to be resolved or how long this will take.

He reaches for something in the glove compartment and I am afraid that there is some paper that pertains to my case, but instead he takes out a candy bar. My mouth begins to salivate and I am surprised at how hungry I am. He offers some to his aide, who declines, and then he offers some to me. "Yes, I'll just have a little piece." The candy is dry with the flavor of fruit, but the sugar feels good on my tongue.

"And then," he goes on, "there is the problem of the return flight . . ."

"Because there's no flight until next week."

Major Lorenzo smiles. "Yes, that's the other problem."

I ponder this for a moment. It seems to me that I should leave as soon as I can. It's this nagging feeling at the back of my brain, but I know that sooner would be better than later. "Major Lorenzo," I say, "I was just wondering . . ."

"Yes," he says, smiling.

"I was wondering, do I have to go back to where I came from? I mean, couldn't you deport me to Cancún or Jamaica? You have flights that go there all the time and I am sure my company would pay for it." Montego Bay suddenly appeals to me. Or Negril. I'll call Todd and have him fly down with Jessica and meet me. We'll snorkel off Sunrise Cove, eating jerk beef and garlic shrimp at Papa Joe's, shoot pool with the Rastamen at Zulu's. This seems like the thing to do.

Major Lorenzo looks perplexed because it is not up to him if I am to stay or to go. He really is only carrying out orders. The two men exchange glances. "It is not so simple," Major Lorenzo says. The guard with the reflector shades is young and good-looking, and he grins at me in his rearview mirror, but this is not a come-on; it is a complicit smile. Because I have come up with a clever solution to this problem. "There is a possibility . . . ," the Major says. "Let me look into it."

"Cancún," I tell him. "Montego Bay." Or anywhere. If they are going to deport me, I have this feeling that they had better do it soon.

Major Lorenzo nods, but his face is solemn and I feel he knows something he is not telling me. He looks as if he is the deliverer of terrible news, and I think to myself as long as no one mentions Isabel, as long as her name never leaves my lips, I'll get out of here soon.

"All right," Major Lorenzo says as we pull up in front of my hotel, "I'll see what I can do." This time he does not get out of the car when the aide opens my door. He stays inside and gives me a short wave. But I know he is watching me as I walk into the hotel.

When I get upstairs to my room, there is a man literally tapping my phone. He has the phone turned upside down in his hand and he holds a small pencil with which he taps the back of the phone. "Is everything all right?" I ask.

"Oh, yes," he replies. "Just a little static." He taps again, grins at me, then a few moments later he is gone. What is this dime-store novel I'm trapped in? Cheap thrills, low-level espionage. What's next? Laser guns, poison-pen notes, secret missions?

When he leaves, I want to call home, but I hesitate. What have they done to my phone? What would I say? It is three o'clock and I wonder what Todd and Jessica are doing right now. When I am away, he picks her up after school. He is probably getting her a snack—cookies with milk, a slice of pizza.

I phone the operator and ask her to place the call, but she tells me all the circuits to the States are busy. Try back in an hour or so, she says. I plead with her. "Please," I say, "it is very important." I feel desperate to get through, as if my life depends on it, though, of course, I don't think it does.

"I am sorry," she tells me, "but I have no line."

I sit on the edge of the bed, staring at the phone. If I close my eyes, I think I will weep. I can see Todd making a butter-and-sugar sandwich. Jessica has her dolls lined up on the counter. There's Ernestine, Bangor, and Rudy. We don't know where the names come from but Jessica gave them those names as soon as she got the dolls. Ernestine is a black Raggedy Ann that I bought her in Jamaica and that some of our friends think is a voodoo doll. Bangor is a fragile, white thing, the closest in resemblance to Jessica herself. Rudy is a disorderly little boy who gets into trouble for no reason at all.

When it is just the two of them, Todd and Jessica get along fine. They like to make a mess in the kitchen, then soak in a leisurely bath. They like to curl up in pajamas and tell stories.

Domesticity bores me. It's not that being Jessica's mother or being married to Todd bores me. It's the repetition of things. The making of beds, folding clothes. Dusting. Dust, my mother, the nurse, told me once as I watched her do the chores, is 80 percent human skin. I don't like the details of running the house. The things you forgot to get at the store, the missing socks, a bill you didn't pay. The valentines have just come down when the Easter bunny goes up. I never have enough juicers in the house.

There's always something going wrong, something that has to be repaired. I can never just sit and stare out at the oak tree, the way you can in a country inn or a bed-and-breakfast or even an interstate motel, where you can close the door when you leave and someone else will take care of what you've left behind.

I didn't want to buy our house. It was Todd who said we should. He wanted a sound investment, something that was his. Never mind that we couldn't afford anything. Todd said we should pioneer. We bought a handyman's special in a neighborhood that was on the brink of some change that never occurred. We have friends who live in a twelve-room Victorian around the corner and they've been trying to get out for years. Despite the drive-by shootings at the bodega down the street, the "Rest in Peace, Joey" graffiti on the abandoned building on the corner, Todd has done wonders with what we have—knocking down walls, bringing in the light. He's managed to put in new fixtures that look just like the old ones we took out.

Before we bought this house, I dreamed it was on a golf course and filled with flying fish. People kept shouting "fore" as fish splattered against the walls. I'm not sure why I dreamed about a golf course since I haven't played in years, though it was the only thing, along with billiards, that my father ever really taught me. Not that I play either well or even like the game, but I can whack a ball down the fairway with a nice, smooth stroke. Even now, my father's coaching remains emblazoned in my mind. Bend your knees, head down. Eyes on the ball.

When I told Todd I didn't want to buy, he said, "Don't be silly, Maggie, it's just a house." Todd can spend an entire weekend ripping out a bathroom, designing new shelves. I've never seen a man so happy stripping paint. Todd's great invention is what he calls "invisible storage." Cubbyholes, secret compartments, hidden drawers tucked under beds and tables. It is perfect, I suppose, for urban living, but I can never find the things I've put away.

I swore I'd never have a conversation with, let alone be married to, a man who said he wanted a propane gauge on his barbecue. We can talk endlessly about our adjustable mortgage and when to lock in. Once conversion meant to me a religious experience. Now it means thirty-years fixed.

Perhaps that is why I go on these junkets. Perhaps that is how I got here.

Actually, I had to go on this trip. That is, I had to get away. I had to get away because something is wrong and I can't quite put my finger on it, though I've searched my house for clues. Clear indicators. A letter, a message, a bill from a hotel. Evidence of Todd's betrayal. Proof that he is drifting away. I want something concrete, something I can sink my teeth into.

It's not exactly that anything happened, but it feels as if something has. When I ask Todd about it, he says, "Maggie, it's all in your head." It's true that our life is as it always has been. But it feels different. What is it you call this in astronomy, these imperceptible tugs? Perambulations? A force that is not seen, but exists because of the impact it has on the things around it.

There is a woman in Todd's office, a designer, named Sarah, and sometimes I believe he has fallen in love with her. Not an affair, not some lusty hotel room when he's supposed to be working. But really in love. The way I know he once was with me and I was with him. That blend of danger and excitement. I see it in his eyes when he talks to her on the phone. But when I say to him, even as a tease, "You're in love with Sarah, aren't you?" Todd replies, "Maggie, get a grip on yourself."

It hasn't been that easy. A few weeks before I left on this trip, we had a break-in. I was in my office, working on the ground floor, when I heard a noise. Doors banging, footsteps. The dog began barking, racing up and down the stairs.

I usually don't hear any noise when I work at home. Todd had converted an old storage closet for me on the ground floor, and on days when I don't have to go into the office (about three days a week), I am set up there in my little insulated windowless space, complete with fax-modem and a hookup to the office. Though he has no children of his own, Kurt encourages this kind of flexible working arrangement. I never thought I could be happy in a windowless room, but actually I am. I don't know what time it is or what the weather is outside. There's a clock on the fax, but I only look at it when I think it may be time to get Jessica from school. I am amazed at how much I can enjoy this solitude. Some days I don't even go outside. Todd jokes that I'm like someone with twentieth-century disease—that illness when you are allergic to your environment, its fumes, its toxic waste—who can't cope with synthetic fibers or cleaning fluids. He likes to kid me that nine out of ten people with this illness are women.

I argue that I just like to be free of the chaos of the

house—the dishes that aren't done, the clothes that need to be put away. I can spend hours checking my E-mail, faxing freelancers all over the world who are gathering information for me when I need the name of a hotel in Eboli, ecotourist information on the birds of Madagascar, where you can get the best brik-à-l'oeuf in Tunis.

I can go on for days like this in my little cell because, of course, unlike here, I know I can leave. I always resist going away, but then once I really go, I am gone. It always amazes me when I travel somewhere how easy it is to leave your other life behind. As if it has ceased to exist; as if it has vanished in thin air.

I was in my own world when I heard the banging upstairs. At first I didn't believe that someone was in the house, but the dog kept growling, running up and down the stairs. He's a small dog, built close to the ground, and I never thought he'd be that fierce, but somehow he chased the person out. When I heard the hatch door slam the second time, I called Todd. He told me to leave the house while he called 911.

We live in a neighborhood where drug dealers have their turf one block from ours, and we rarely go out at night. Some of our neighbors have bullet-proof front doors, but so far we had resisted such precautions. But Todd said it was time to put in an alarm system.

Lyle Nashe, the Home Security Alarm salesman who arrived, wore a shiny blue suit and carried a small suitcase. First he admired our house—the banisters Todd had stripped, the marble mantel that had once been covered in blue paint. He said, "You've done wonders with this place," winning Todd over, but not me. He liked the country kitchen, the primitive art on the walls that I bring back from wherever I go. "I like it," Lyle Nashe said. "It's eclectic. You have a lot you must want to protect here."

"Actually," I told him, "our possessions don't amount to much. We just want to feel safe."

"Well, I think I have the right system for you." He put his suitcase on the table. It had two doors that opened like an advent calendar, revealing a miniature house, complete with a pot on the stove, crib in the nursery, dog on the stairs who Jessica thought resembled Sandy, which is our dog's name, like Little Orphan Annie's.

Then Lyle Nashe produced a tiny masked man carrying a burglar bag whom he moved from a window, onto the roof, and then down the back stairs. The movable burglar had a mustache and wore a black cap. He was dark-complected, but not black. Racially diverse, I categorized him. "These are your vulnerable spots," Lyle Nashe told us, "your potential danger situations. This is where trouble begins."

Todd and I followed Lyle Nashe's long fingers as the masked man peered into windows, crept down the back stairs. Lyle Nashe outlined all the dangers—the things that could happen. He suggested motion detectors, raised above the level of the dog, which wasn't very high, he noted, as he assessed Sandy. Panic buttons in all the bedrooms that would shine red in the night. He told us that if we were in a hostage situation with a gun to our heads and a maniac telling us to disarm the system, we could just punch in our code back-ward. "Believe me, the police will come."

Lyle Nashe snapped shut the door of his miniature crime demonstration. "You can't imagine the things I've seen. Last month I did an installation for a widow. Her husband had died a few weeks before. She'd woken one morning to find a man with a wire, standing over her bed. The widow doesn't know what made her do this, but she shouted out, 'John, get the gun; there's a man in the house.' The cat heard her and knocked something over downstairs. The man fled."

Todd wanted the entire system—the motion detectors, the panic buttons, the grates on the skylight. We put in a steel hatch with a spring door and bars on the skylight Todd had carved out himself. The shadows on the ceiling look like prison windows. "I want you to feel safe." At night we put the system on "home," but I always forget it is on in the morning when I open the back door to let Sandy out. Alarm central is always calling, asking for my password. "Ninja," I say, which is the word Jessica thought up.

Todd likes to put the system on test so we can run through our practice drills. "Pretend you're in a hostage situation, Maggie, and someone has a gun to your head." I punch in the code backward, but I have an odd feeling that this turns Todd on. At night in bed, I've whispered to him, "Todd, get the gun; there's a man in the house." He laughs, but soon his laugh turns to sighs and he is all over me.

For days after the break-in I trembled at the slightest sound. I envisioned the man who had broken in coming down the stairs, a crowbar in his hand. I always pictured the little burglar from Lyle Nashe's model house—a man in a black cap, a Lone Ranger mask with a black mustache. Slightly dark-complected—Hispanic, not black. We confront each other on the stairs. He carries his burglar bag like a doctor on a home visit.

Once I took a self-defense class ("Women and Power," it was called) and was told that if a woman is being attacked or taken against her will, it helps if she acts insane or growls like an animal. Urinating is also effective.

At night Todd reaches across, cradling me in his arms. He

has long, taut arms that engulf me. The muscles on his back are sturdy. I can trace a butterfly. "You're safe, Maggie," Todd tells me when he finds me trembling. "Everything's all right." His kisses are deep and soothing. I rarely say no.

So why don't I feel safe? I wonder.

Fourteen

I T WAS RAINING when I saw Isabel again. I had tried for a few days not to see her, going about my work, visiting the cigar museum, the sugarcane plant, the newly renovated plastic-surgery hospital where women were having face-lifts. Then she phoned. "It's me," she said, "there's going to be a storm, so you can't go out. Let me come and see you at the hotel." An hour later the skies opened into a torrential downpour and Isabel raced into the lobby, drenched, a newspaper over her head. Her red dress clung to her thighs, her nipples stood erect as she came in laughing, shaking her body like a dog.

"You're soaked," I told her, "You need something else to wear."

"Yes, that would be nice." She squeezed the water from her hair as if she were wringing a towel.

"Come upstairs. I'll loan you something." Isabel looked me up and down. "A T-shirt," I said, "a skirt. You need to get out of your wet things."

As we rode the elevator to my room, we could hear the thunder roar. "The gods are angry," Isabel said. Inside my room was dark and outside the wind blew, rattling the shutters. I told Isabel to go into the bathroom and dry off and I'd hand her some things. But she protested. "No, I want to see all your clothes. I want you to model them for me."

"Don't be silly."

"No, please, I want to see everything you have."

"Well, here," I said, handing her an oversize T-shirt from Puerto Vallarta. "At least for now, put this on." Isabel went into the bathroom. I could hear the sound of a towel rubbing against skin, a toilet flushing. While I waited, I gazed outside. Rain poured down into the narrow sidestreets, sending rivulets along the gutters. The sky was dark, black, almost as if it were the end of the world.

It seemed a long time before Isabel came out of the bathroom. She had twisted her hair up into a knot on the top of her head. My T-shirt just barely covered her thighs as she stretched out across my bed. "Okay, let's do a fashion show. I want to see all your clothes."

"But I've hardly brought anything down with me."

Isabel rose from the bed, "Oh, come on now. I like this pink jumpsuit." She was opening my closet, peering in. "I like this." She pulled out a black cotton dress that I sometimes wear to travel in, and another with a floral print. "Oh, model for me." She laughed.

Flopping back down on the bed, she cocked her head. I was embarrassed getting undressed with her in the light of day so I took the black dress off its hanger and slipped into the bathroom, where I quickly stepped into the dress and a pair of black sandals. I dabbed on lipstick for good measure, some perfume behind my ears. Then exited the bathroom with some flourish.

"Yes," Isabel clapped. "Brava. Turn around, turn. Oh, you have great hips. Nice shape. You'll go dancing with me tonight in that." She jumped up, started scurrying around on my closet floor. "Let's see. Not sandals. Another kind of shoes. Oh, I love these little red shoes." She tried to slip them on, but her feet were much larger than mine and after a struggle she gave up. "You'll wear these red shoes tonight." I knew I didn't really have time to go out dancing with her that evening. I didn't even have time to be in the room with her trying on clothes. I had a five-page list of things to do, places I needed to see. But somehow that list meant less and less to me, and I found that world of responsibility and assignments and all those things I had to do drifting farther and farther behind.

"Now let me see you," Isabel said, lying down on the bed. "Turn a little. Black eyeliner and your hair pulled back, off your ears, what do you think?" She tucked my hair behind my ears, then leaned back, satisfied. "There." Stretching her long legs out, she raised her arms over her head. "We'll go to the Palacio de Salsa. Dance the merengue." She jumped off the bed and began to do what I assume was the merengue around the room, eyes closed, one hand resting on her belly, the other on an imaginary partner. She headed toward my closet, where she began once again to rifle through my things, pulling out a pink jumpsuit, shaking her head. "Oh, I like this," she said, pausing at a floral dress. "Here, put this on."

Just then the phone rang, startling both of us. Isabel looked at the phone askance, as if she had never seen one before, then pointed for me to answer it. "It's for you," Isabel said, as if it could be for anyone else.

"Maggie . . ." I heard the crackling sound of long distance. "It's me." It took me a moment to recognize his voice, but it was Todd. "I was just taking a chance. I'm glad you're in."

Isabel gave me a little wave, slinked off the bed, and began opening my drawers. I motioned for her to stop, but she winked and went on. "Is anything wrong?"

"No, does something have to be wrong?" He sounded a little hurt. "I just wanted to hear your voice."

"Oh, well, I'm fine. Busy. Just catching up on some notes." I looked at my notes, neatly stacked, the pile of what I had accomplished, significantly smaller than the one I should have had. "Everything okay?"

"Oh, as well as can be expected without you here."

"I miss you guys too," I said, gazing at Isabel, who was taking my Victoria's Secret purple nightgown out of the drawer, holding it up to herself. She ran her hands along its smooth satin, gave her hips a shake.

"I got a note from the school today," Todd went on.

"The school?" I panicked.

"Oh, it's no big deal. They said we missed a tuition payment in December, but I thought you'd paid it."

"Maybe I forgot."

"You forgot?" The tension rose in his voice. We divide our tasks carefully. He walks the dog; I make breakfast. I shop for produce; he buys staples. Here was a domestic task for which I was responsible—short-term finances, we called it, which meant bills, one of which was for Jessica's private-school tuition.

Of course, we didn't want her to go to private school. We

had resisted because we both had public-school educations and we believed in it, but given our neighborhood and all the cuts (our school district didn't have an art teacher until last January and then only because the PTA paid for it), in the end it seemed inevitable that she would have to go to the private school near our house, which was where all our friends' children went.

Still it was a sacrifice, financially I mean. Perhaps I hadn't paid December because our bills seemed very tight around Christmas. Or perhaps I'd just forgotten. But somehow in that hotel room with a blackened sky outside and the rain cascading down and Isabel going through my dresser drawers, examining my clothes, I didn't seem to care. "Look, can you just pay it?"

"Of course I can, but . . ."

"Todd, is this why you called me?"

"No, I said I wanted to hear your voice."

"Yes, well, I've wanted to hear yours as well." Now Isabel had taken other clothes out of my drawers—a slip she seemed to like, a silk pantsuit. A sweater of silvery cotton that she held up to herself in front of the mirror. "Nice," she mouthed to me. I stifled a giggle, turning away from her.

"Maggie, you seem distracted. Is anyone else there?"

"Well, yes, a friend."

"What kind of friend?"

"A woman I know." Isabel was taking off the T-shirt I'd given her, slipping my cotton sweater on. It was too short-waisted so she picked up the Victoria's Secret nightgown again and danced past me around the room, my nightgown held across her chest.

"Well, then, I won't keep you." His voice relaxed; now he was somewhat reassured.

"Yes, I probably should go." And then I asked him, "Is there anything else I forgot?"

"Yes, you forgot to say that you love me."

"I love you," I whispered into the receiver, not wanting Isabel to hear, though the words had little resonance for me at that moment as Isabel puckered her lips and blew me a kiss. "I love you too," she whispered, then turned away from me, laughing.

"You're terrible," I said when I got off the phone. She shook her head, peevishly, still holding the nightgown. "If you really like that, you can keep it. I can get another one."

She clasped it to her, smiling. "Oh, do you mean it?"

"Of course I mean it," I said, wondering what I'd tell Todd when he asked me where it was.

"So, I'm going to go now and get ready for tonight. What time shall I pick you up?"

"Eight o'clock," I told her.

"Good," she said, smiling, kissing me on the cheek. "Be downstairs."

Though I was downstairs at eight, Isabel arrived just before nine with a flurry of apologies and we went off to the Palacio de Salsa, where the music blared and Isabel danced in the strobe for hours without stopping. She danced with me, and then she danced with anyone who would dance with her— and there were many who wanted to. Her body shook in an odd, frenzied way, oblivious to her partner or to whether or not I was with her. Sometime after midnight I walked out of the disco without saying good-bye.

The next day I went looking for Isabel. Of course, I had a million things to do, but I was concerned that she had gotten home all right and felt bad that I'd left her there alone, so instead of doing what I needed to do, I took a cab to her apartment. When I rang, Milagro answered, the scent of incense (eucalyptus, perhaps, or cedar) wafting around her, dressed in a T-shirt and shorts that were tight for her. Music blared in the background. "I was hoping to find your mother."

Milagro made a face, pointing inside to where the music was too loud. She disappeared, turned it off, then came back to me again. "She's out, but please, come in," Milagro said, leading me across the flower petals that were sprinkled on the floor. "Would you like something to drink?"

"Yes, I would, it's very warm."

She opened the refrigerator, which was filled with packages of cheese, chocolate, and soft drinks. "It's so good of you to come and see us. You have been so nice to Mummy." Milagro poured me a glass of Fanta, a drink that I detest. I sipped it slowly as she sat across from me on the sofa, drinking the rest out of the bottle. I sat in a large, soft chair.

"Well, I wish I could do more."

Milagro sighed. "Oh, it's not easy. Mummy is so unhappy. Everything is so terrible for her here."

"Yes, she seems sad."

Milagro wiped her brow with her hand. I had the feeling she had been dancing alone in the apartment. "I wish she could leave. I want her to go away."

"You want your mother to go away?"

"Of course, I want to be with her, but she needs to get away."

"Yes, I can see that she does . . ." I glanced around the apartment at the pictures on the walls, the windows open, the breeze blowing in. "This is a nice apartment," I said. "It's cozy."

"We do the best we can," Milagro said with the wry smile I'd seen on her mother's lips many times before.

The sweetness of the Fanta stuck to my mouth. Suddenly I felt awkward being there, as if I was spying on them. Perhaps in some way I was. I rose without finishing the drink. "I must get going."

"I'll tell Mummy you stopped by."

"Yes, please do that." As soon as Milagro closed the door, salsa once again blared from inside the apartment, and in the window I could see her shadow, dancing. I paused for a moment in the overgrown garden, thinking about all the things I'd pull out if it were my garden. The weeping bottlebrush and the hibiscus were dwarfed by the giant screw pine that extended its tentacles through the garden. High in its branches I saw a white bird-of-paradise, its petals about to bloom.

Fifteen

IN THE EVENING Manuel comes to have dinner with me at the hotel. He is dressed in a linen jacket, tie, white shirt. His hair is slicked back with Brylcreem like a gangster. "Oh, you look beautiful," he says. "I love this cream-colored jumpsuit." He touches it with his hand, runs the fabric between his fingers. "I wish I could take you out to El Colibrí, then dancing at the Club Tropical," he says, escorting me with a moist palm on my waist into the restaurant in the lobby, "but this will have to do." El Colibrí is the only restaurant where dollars and pesos mix. It also serves the best rice, beans, and *ropa vieja* around, but I have to settle for dinner within the confines of the hotel.

The hotel restaurant is virtually empty and the waiters mill in the corners. On the menu there are scant offerings—a fried chicken dish, a seafood salad that I had for lunch. "Why don't we try the roof terrace?" Manuel suggests, closing his menu. Nodding to the waiters, who shrug with indifferent smiles, he guides me to the narrow elevator, which climbs slowly to the sixth floor. The numbers in the elevator are set wrong and we cannot tell what floor we are on.

The elevator doors open to a roof illuminated with strings of Christmas lights. We take a table near the bar and both order the lamb on the spit. The lamb is scrawny, so it shouldn't take that long to cook. It is a balmy night and Manuel orders two daiquiris. We sit at a dimly lit table, listening to the crackle as the grease falls into the fire. Looking up, I see a half-moon over the city. A gentle sea breeze blows through the palm fronds on the deck.

"Do you think," Manuel asks, pressing his mouth to my ear, "that it's safe to talk here?" I decide I better get used to whispering. I tell him I don't know. I'm not sure what safe is anymore, but I'm pretty certain that the roof is better than my room. "It took them two hours to get the room ready. Believe me, it doesn't take two hours to make a bed."

"I want to know whatever you can tell me. What do you think has happened to you?"

I tell him that I was stopped at the airport and not allowed in, that after a night they brought me here. That a man named Major Lorenzo is in charge of getting me home. But today they questioned me all morning about whom I met the last time I was here.

"And did you mention anyone?" Manuel asks, a tremor to his voice.

"No, I said I didn't remember who I met."

Manuel nods. "They must think you are a spy," he says matter-of-factly.

"Me?" I laugh, though this does not strike me as funny.

"Yes, they are treating you decently for now, but they probably suspect you of spying."

"But I'm not . . ."

"Of course." Manuel pats my hand. "We know that. You must convince them."

Despite its scrawniness, our lamb is slow to cook. Manuel and I watch it turning on the spit, the fat dripping down. Music comes on, a lively salsa beat, from the speaker beside our table. The group is Calle Ocho, Manuel informs me, named for the street in Miami's Little Havana where they originate. Pirated music, Manuel says. "Dance with me." He takes me in his arms and we dance, our cheeks pressed together.

He seems to be all arms, like an octopus, and I never know where a hand will appear next. On my bottom, on the side of my breast. I try to push them down, but they only reappear. We are about the same height and I can smell the pomade in his hair. His arms are stronger than I'd imagined and he holds me so hard I can scarcely breathe. "I've missed you," he says. "Two years is a long time."

The waiter signals that our lamb is done and I pull away, leading Manuel back to our table. The lamb looks sinewy and underfed, more like a roadkill than a meal. I poke it with my fork, not at all sure I can eat. "Do you think," I ask Manuel hesitantly, "that they know about what happened between me and Isabel?"

Manuel picks up his fork, sampling his lamb. "Probably," he says. "I think they must."

"I'm afraid," I tell him, "I really am." I breathe a deep sigh, thinking Lydia was right. I was stupid to come back. "But will they let me go?" I ask, truly frightened for the first time.

He smiles. "Oh, I'm pretty sure they will. They are just trying to teach you a lesson." He takes a bite, though he does not seem very interested in the meal.

"What has happened to her?" I ask him. "Why hasn't she ever written to me?"

"Oh, my guess is that she wants to put it all behind her. She is just living her life." I am shaking my head and he touches my cheek. "You know," he says, "I still want you. Nothing has changed." He puts down his fork. "Come," he says, "dance with me again."

The music is a pretty good salsa and Manuel definitely knows the beat. I am less sure of it, but he is the kind of dancer who could guide a moose around a dance floor. His feet slide and manage to bring me along, and whenever I miss a step, he fills it in for me. He can switch his samba to a rumba to the mambo without skipping a beat. Todd can dance American-style from the sixties, where you never touch, but Manuel knows how to guide a woman along the floor. We pause only for another round of daiquiris while the kids at the bar put on a new tape and then we rumba around the roof deck again.

It is late when Manuel walks me to my room. My muscles ache from the dancing and my head spins from the daiquiris, but Manuel wants to come inside my room. I tell him no, that I want him to go home, but he wants to come inside. We have both had too much to drink, he more than I, but I am sober enough to know that I do not want him in my room. I had a very pleasant evening, I tell him, though of course I paid for it, and I am hoping he can help me get home but I cannot let him come in. You must go, I tell him, bracing the door with my foot. His cigarette smoke curls in the air between us as he tries to convince me otherwise.

Of course, Manuel wants to sleep with me and I cannot say that I would not like to sleep with him. But I know what my main attraction is; it is my resistance. My refusal. I will go so far, but not far enough. In this way I am chaste and true to my marriage. I cannot live feeling that I have something to confess.

Manuel thrusts his face close to mine, asking one more time if he can stay and I am tempted to say yes. His hands touch my face, my neck, but I tell him no, pushing the door closed. He must leave. I listen for a few moments as he stands outside, deciding what to do next. Then I hear his footsteps as he shuffles away.

I crawl into my narrow bed. It is odd to be sleeping alone. I am used to bodies in the bed—husband, child, dog. I curl up, trying to imagine that Jessica is there. I am the one who puts her to bed at night. She wraps her arms around my neck and holds me there until she is asleep. Often I fall asleep as well and Todd has to come and wake me. He nudges me until I stumble into bed. When Jessica was born, I counted all her fingers and her toes. I checked to see she had all her parts. Now at this distance I try to remember her child's body, miniature arms and legs. I sniff for her odor. I try to reconstruct her, piece by piece.

The room smells of Manuel's cigarette smoke and of the pomade he puts on his hair. The sheets that had been so cool and comforting to me before begin to itch. I get up and throw open the balcony doors. It is a beautiful night—balmy and clear. I take a deep breath. Then, clasping the railing of the balcony, I peer down.

Music comes from somewhere, salsa with that strong Latin beat, and I tap my fingers. In the plaza below dozens of people mill about. Lovers kiss on the banquettes beneath the waving palmettos. Men with beer bottles play cards under a streetlight. But mainly what I feel are bodies. It is as if I can smell them up here. Warm bodies, bodies that will mingle and blend. Skin will rub against sticky skin on this warm night. Closing my eyes, I try to imagine hands on my breasts, my hips. A tongue gliding over my body, dipping into my openings, my cracks.

Sixteen

THE NIGHT before I left, Todd wanted to make love. When I crawled into bed beside him, he reached for me. Usually we at least read for a little while, but that night he immediately turned to me. His hands seemed to be all over me, on my thighs, my buttocks, my breasts. He pulled me to him as if somehow he were afraid I'd disappear. I lay back and let him do the work. His fingers reached inside of me; I felt his tongue gliding down my thigh. "Relax, Maggie," he said. "Don't try so hard."

"I'm relaxed," I said, but my mind was on other things. What had I forgotten? Had I packed too much? Should I bring more for gifts and bribes—soap, toothpaste, canned goods? Pencils, Chiclets? Who would take Jessica to gymnastics on Tuesday? Was that on my list for Todd?

The covers came off and suddenly I was cold. Shivering, I folded my hands across my chest. Todd pulled away, rising out of the bed. "I don't know where you are, Maggie, but it's not with me."

Sometimes I think I invent these little tests just to see if he's paying attention, if he really notices me.

Todd and I met at a Valentine's ball. It's not the kind of thing I'd normally attend, but it was Valentine's and my girlfriend Betsy and her husband Wade, who were throwing it, wanted me to come. Be coy, she told me. Flirt.

When I arrived I found a room full of people dressed in red and black, all in black masks. I'd read once in a biology book that red and black in the animal world are the colors of venom. I've never done well in crowds, let alone in crowds of masked strangers, and I drifted to a corner of the room, where a man leaned against the wall.

He wore a black shirt and pants and the two of us looked as if somebody had died. I couldn't see his face, but I noticed his long, slim hands. They were white and delicate, as if he played the piano. I thought it would be nice to be touched by those hands. I felt foolish wearing a mask and feared it would leave strange creases on my face, like a raccoon.

"I haven't worn a mask since I thought I was the Lone Ranger" were the first words he said to me. We both started to laugh.

When we left together, he asked if I wanted to share a cab. In the cab he asked if I wanted to stop by his place for a drink. I know this scenario, I told myself, I've been here before. "Sure," I said, "why not." When we got there, he lifted off my mask to kiss me. Then he said, jokingly, I liked you better with your mask on.

What's that supposed to mean? I asked.

We began to see each other a few times a week. When we went out, he'd come over early and fix things around my apartment. He screwed hooks on the wall so I could hang up my bathrobe. He put in shelves beside my bed, happily puttering around. Sometimes on a Saturday afternoon we just stayed inside and I'd read and listen to music and he'd put new faucets on the sink.

It took a while before he told me that he was seeing someone else. A woman from his office. Not Sarah, but someone who left shortly after we got married. He said it wasn't serious with her, but it had been going on for a long time. For weeks he was torn between the two of us. He'd see me one night and her the next. On the nights when he didn't see me, I found myself walking down the street where he lived. I'd look up at his apartment to see if there was a light on. Once I saw the shadows of two people against the wall.

After that I stopped returning his calls. He wrote me a note to ask what was wrong. I waited a few weeks, then I wrote him back. I told him I liked the way he laughed and the way he knew how everything worked. He could tell me how my toaster worked, how water moved through the pipes in the kitchen. If you ever stop seeing the woman in your office, I wrote to him, I'd love to see you again. Two weeks later we were together and since then we haven't been apart.

Before meeting Todd, I moved around a great deal. I was restless, though I couldn't tell you why. I lived in different places—a lot of them, really—and never had, or wanted, much that was my own. I lived in the Bay Area for a while and liked it there, where I worked for a start-up magazine called *On the Road*, but it folded after a year, and that and an earthquake shattered my confidence. I went up to Seattle, but the weather got me down and no one laughed at my jokes. I didn't want to come back East, but that was where the magazine jobs were.

My first job was writing the honeymoon column for *Bride Magazine*. I traveled to five-star resorts all over the world and stayed alone in honeymoon suites. You might think this would be an interesting job, finding romantic destinations for newlyweds—an Australian outback ranch overrun with marsupials, a hotel on Maui whose rooms were accessible only by launch, the concierge floor at the Peninsula in Los Angeles— but actually it was very lonely. I had everything at my fingertips, never had to leave the room.

I became adept at assessing comfort—the coolness of the sheets, the seclusion of the room, the speed of room service. I learned to distinguish good food from bad and warned love-hungry couples of heavy sauces, overcooked meat. Then I'd fly home, where I had short-lived relationships with fly-by-night men. Some lasted a few weeks, others a season. There was one man I liked very much who took me ice-skating at Rockefeller Center on Christmas Eve; then I never saw him again. A man named Dan who made documentaries lasted over a year, until he came down with a venereal disease he did not get from me. Another waited until I'd fallen in love with him, then took an assignment abroad.

Todd seemed to enjoy my comings and goings. He liked to think of me as some kind of an adventurer, which I was not and really am not. After a long weekend alone in a feather bed in Ravello, Todd had dinner cooking for us on the stove. I thought I could get used to this—the comfort of familiar things. Over steaks and wine he asked me if I didn't want to think about settling down and I told him I did.

The night before I left on this trip, Todd stood at the window, his buttocks white, his body lean. I have always admired his long lines, his gazellelike stride. Now he stood still, alert, watching something.

I got up, naked as well, and stood at the window beside him. The sky was a startling white and from it huge flakes fell. Big, billowy flakes, covering the back garden, the garbage, and the filth. I've never much enjoyed the feeling of being snowbound, stuck inside. You can't go to work. You can barely trudge to the store. Todd put a cold hand on my shoulder and for once it was my turn to warm him.

"Maybe I won't be able to leave," I told him.

Now he tipped my head back. "I wish that were so."

This time he had my attention. Maybe I won't be able to go anywhere, maybe I'll just stay cocooned inside. I brought him back to the warmth of our bed. For once I was the one who was all over him. My hands on his nipples, my head bent between his legs. He groaned, tossing his head from side to side, but my mind was elsewhere. I was already gone.

We woke to the scraping of shovel to asphalt. As I left for the airport, our neighbor, Joel Rodgers, stood with his thermos of hot chocolate laced with brandy, offering it to every passerby, and Pete Bennett, who lived across the street, had his salt and state-of-the-art stainless steel shovel, which he proudly displayed.

Teenage boys from farther down the block were coming by, offering their services. On a summer's night they play their music too loud. There have been muggings down the block, so I try to stay above Fourth Avenue. But in winter for a few dollars these kids will shovel us out. Todd gave them five bucks as we left. Todd and Jessica both took me—they insisted on taking me—to the airport. In the taxi we huddled together like bears in a cave. First I'd fly to Miami. There I'd get the plane to *la isla*. "Bring me saltwater taffy, Mommy," Jessica said. "Bring the warm weather home," Todd said, smiling, kissing me lightly on the lips.

Somewhere over the Carolinas, as coffee was being served, I see Jessica and Todd building a snowman out front. They're heating the lentil soup I've left them and hot chocolate on the stove. Now someone has brought out a sled and everyone is piling on. Jessica gets her little green sled out too. All the children go sledding down the middle of the street, striking terror in their parents' hearts, as if suddenly a car will materialize in this snowy scene, a snowplow will appear out of the blue, and a parent's face will round into a scream as a child sleds downhill.

Seventeen

BEHIND THE HOUSE where I grew up there was a creek and it was the nicest thing about where we lived. It was called Indian River and Lydia and I went there whenever we could. We started going so we could let our mother sleep. Along Indian Creek there was a path and we followed it as far as we dared into the woods. We'd head out on a fall day, listening to every rustle, imagining we saw deer or even bear. We'd walk for a long time until it got dark. Then we'd follow the thread of the stream back toward our house.

I never enjoyed the walk back. I wanted to keep going, farther and deeper into the woods. If it hadn't been for Lydia, I probably would have, though she never asked me to turn around. Our house sat on top of a knoll and I liked to stand at the edge of the creek and look at the house, wondering what kind of people lived inside. I imagined pots of savory stew, hot on the stove, a fireplace with a fire burning. A father reading a book in his chair with a cat or dog at his feet. I wanted to pass this house and go on to the next, but Lydia would take my hand and lead me home.

We tiptoed into the house because our mother slept in the afternoons. For years she worked as a graveyard nurse because the pay was better. When I was small, I thought this meant she took care of sick people in cemeteries. She worked at night, tending the needs of the sleeping and comatose, handing out pills, giving shots, comforting them in their night terrors while her own children—Lydia and myself—waved good-bye to her as she came in each morning and we headed off to school.

During the day she slept. I have learned to open a refrigerator without making a sound, to watch television with no volume, as if the actors were mute. We whispered when we spoke because if we woke our mother she would be angry. She never screamed at us, but if we bothered her she made us go with our father to the store.

After the plastic business went bankrupt, my father opened a card and stationery shop at the mall on the outskirts of the town where we lived near the Canadian border. The shop was divided into occasions—birthdays, Halloween, religious. When Lydia and I played in the store, we liked to mix up the envelopes so that the wrong size would be with the wrong card. Our father was often talking to suppliers, and later to his creditors, and we'd hear him shouting, "I want aunts, I want uncles, I want sympathy."

Our father never really seemed to like it when we were there. He had business to tend to and he was always on the phone, his hand cupped around the receiver. I remember trying to read his lips. Sometimes he gave us things to do. He let us use the adding machine. Once he gave us a pad of white paper and colored pens and we made pictures that he hung up behind the cash register.

Lydia always brought her dolls with her. I had dolls too but mine sat on a shelf in our room. Lydia carried hers around in a small suitcase like the sample cases of the salesmen who frequented the store. She lined them up on the counter and pretended they were customers. The dolls would buy reams of paper, a million envelopes, and we'd never have to worry about money again. Though there were never many people in the store, our father couldn't seem to stand our voices, and our laughter made him scowl. If we giggled or made noise, he shook a fist at us as if he would hit us. He never did, but it seemed as if he would.

At night while our mother worked the graveyard shift, our father stayed in his room illuminated by the blue light of the TV and Lydia dressed and undressed her dolls. We could hear the TV seep into our room all night long—the blare of bargain sales, late-night talk shows, swashbuckling films. Before Lydia went to sleep, she played with her dolls. She liked to dress them up, comb their hair. Fix them up as if they had parties to go to, places to be. She made them plaid skirts and gypsy turbans, serapes and cowgirl suits out of bits of scrap.

While she groomed her dolls, I sat on my bed and we spoke softly in the secret language that only we understood. Actually, even we didn't understand it, but we memorized phrases and words that meant things like "Do you want a chicken sandwich?" or "Do you think you'll get an A in algebra?" and we'd understand. Once Lydia wanted me to come up with a word for mad. She was angry and said she wanted to say, "I am mad." But I told her that the word didn't exist. No one who spoke our language was ever mad.

If our father heard us talking in our language, he'd make us sleep apart. There was a guest room (not that we ever had any guests, but later our mother slept there) and he'd make Lydia sleep in that room. He said, "You girls are being bad again. You are very bad."

Before he put Lydia in the guest room, he took her dolls away. Lydia begged him not to, but he said that when she was good, she could have them back again.

Because our mother slept in the afternoon, it was usually our father who attended school assemblies and plays. He went to school dressed in a suit and tie. There was something dashing about him when he came for our school plays. Once we did all the states in the union. I was West Virginia and Lydia was Oregon. The presentations went east to west and our father had to sit through all the states in between.

Our teacher, Miss Debencorn, seemed to like our father. She brought him little cups of apple juice, which he refused, shaking his head. But they kept talking, their heads leaned together, laughing from time to time. Miss Debencorn must have thought he was raising us on his own. As we were leaving school that day, our father took us each by the arm. "Yes," he said, "they're great little girls."

In the car home he said he was very proud of us and Lydia asked if we could stop for ice cream. He said no, he wanted to get home, but she asked again. She said if he was so proud of us, why couldn't we stop for ice cream. I nudged her and told her to stop, but Lydia could be like a Gila monster and never let go. "I'm not driving five miles out of my way for ice cream," he said, his voice rising, and I elbowed Lydia, but she wouldn't stop. She pleaded with him to take us. So he pulled the car over and took her dolls and put them in the trunk. "You are being very bad," he told her. "When you are good, you can have them back."

Lydia kept asking if she were good enough, but it would be weeks before she got her dolls back again. I asked him if he'd take something of mine, but he said, "No, Maggie. Nothing matters that much to you."

He was always threatening to leave. He'd say, If you girls do this one more time, I'm out of here. Sometimes he threatened to leave when our mother was at work, and that was the most frightening. Lydia would howl and beg.

Once he actually left. It was during a snowstorm and he said we'd been bad and he wasn't going to stay. There was a blizzard outside as he headed out to the garage. I put on my coat and boots and chased after him, but the snow was so deep I almost lost my way. I found myself literally following in his footsteps, placing one foot carefully into the impressions he'd made. But when I got to the garage, he was gone.

Eighteen

THE BEAUTICIAN'S NAME is Olga and she asks me what I'd like to have done. She has a lacquered beehive, the kind I haven't seen since the sixties, and painted-on eyebrows. "I'd like you to do my nails," I say. I extend my brittle, bitten fingers and Olga winces, turning away.

She is finishing up a client and apologizes for the wait. "That's all right," I tell her. "I'm not in a rush." The beauty shop is all windows and I can sit in this kind of glass fishbowl and watch for Major Lorenzo here. Olga suggests I look at the colors. She hands me magazines with assorted designs. The woman in the chair is a German tourist and is having one of those designer manicures—green and orange swirls, pearly tips. Black glitter is sprinkled on. I wonder if I dare go this far; would Major Lorenzo think I've gone off the deep end? Would Todd think I'd lost my mind when I came home?

The last time I got my nails done was for my wedding. My mother set me up with her beautician, a dour woman named

Corinne. My mother told me that you can judge a woman by her nails. Corinne filed mine to claws and told me to go catch my prey. I had a friend named Esther who had perfect nails. They were amazing—long, perfect, ruby red. Esther began doing her nails when her mother was dying and Esther lost her job. She said she found she couldn't do anything to take care of herself, but she could do her nails. After that she decided to keep doing them. As long as my nails are done, Esther told me, I know I'm hanging on.

Olga works intently on the tourist's nails, which seem to take a long time. I imagine fairy tales recounted into her tips—Hansel and Gretel again comes to mind, Little Red Riding Hood. Woodsy stories in line with current modes. As Olga works away in an intense silence, I leaf through the local couture magazine. Neo–cavewoman seems to be the latest thing. Women in furry fringe, tiger suits, shaggy, torn fur. In a country where there are no imports and no exports, the theme seems to be back to the woods. Or for women, at least, back to the cave.

Though I can't remember seeing a motorcycle on *la isla*, a model stands before one on a dirt road. Leafs and twigs hang from their hair, her face is covered with soot, and she has a dead look to her eyes. She looks as if she has just been gang-raped on the soft shoulder. I look more closely until I see through the leaves and twigs and dirt and realize that the woman standing in front of the motorcycle is Isabel. She is all made-up and her hair falls wildly around her, but there is no mistaking those dark features, the distant look that gazes beyond the page. I check the date on the magazine and it is from two years ago and I have not laid eyes on her in just as long.

The German woman holds up her nails, smiling happily.

She blows on them in short, hearty puffs, displaying them for me to see. There are no fairy tales here, just swirls and sprinkles in black and red. She tips Olga in deutsche marks and the beautician pockets the money, discreetly checking the amount.

Hastily I close the magazine as Olga motions for me to sit down at her little table. As I wait while she changes the towel and the water, I feel strangely disoriented, as if I have been awakened suddenly and don't know where I am. She brings a small plastic tub with fresh warm water and soap and again motions for me to stick one of my hands in and I feel powerless to do anything other than what she commands. In her dark red claws she picks up my other hand. She stares with a look of disdain at nails broken, chewed down, brittle, the result of years of worry and work. I chew anything I can— pens, gum, carrots, my nails.

"Tsk, tsk," Olga says. "You should take better care of your hands." My hands, my hair, my body, my head, my heart, the whole thing, I want to tell her, but who am I to confide in her?

"So," she says, "are you enjoying it here? Do you like your visit so far?"

"Oh, yes," I tell her. "Everything is wonderful."

"And what have you seen?"

I make it all up. The churches, the fortress, the zoo. Why do I suspect she is being paid to ask these questions? How could this nice woman doing my nails be an informer? But I feel certain she is, like everyone who works in the hotel.

I decide to call her bluff. "You know, back home, in the United States, people say that you don't have anything here. That you can't get goods; that you are not free."

"That is not true. No one is starving; we can work if we

choose. You have people who sleep in your streets; you have people who die of the cold."

"Yes, but we are free," I tell her.

"Free to do what?" Olga asks, filing my nails a little too briskly. At any moment I expect them to bleed.

"So you are happy."

"Of course I am happy. I love it here," Olga tells me. "I love our leader. I hope he lives for twenty more years."

"Why do you love him?"

"Because he has given us everything—I have food, a place to live, a job. People who say otherwise are just lazy. They don't want to work for this country. They are spoiled children who only know how to complain. They don't realize the gift they've been given."

"Where do you live?" I ask her.

"Oh," she says, with a whirl of her hand, "it is far away." This is what people from *la isla* say when they want to make sure you won't come to their house. I smile at the irony; don't worry, I want to add, you can't take me there, even if you wanted to. "What color?" she asks.

There are only three or four colors, outside of the green and orange and black. There's a pearly pink, which seems too muted, given the circumstances, and a nice copper, if I had a tan. In the end I can't choose so I let Olga decide for me.

She picks out ruby red. I watch as with a sure, even stroke she paints my nails red as blood.

Major Lorenzo can't be more than ten years older than me. I wonder what he thinks as he enters the lobby of the hotel. He waves as if he is glad to see me. I wave back, thinking this will help my nails dry more quickly. As I approach, I am hoping he has some news.

He extends his hand to shake mine, but I point to my nails. "Manicure," I say with a grin and he laughs, finding me amusing. I wonder what he really thinks. Does he see an attractive young woman in her prime or an enemy of the state? Would he try to sleep with me in another moment under other circumstances? Or am I just a problem he has to deal with? Paperwork. A person to process, then get on to the next thing.

I am not a counterrevolutionary, I want to explain. I'm not even a journalist. I am just a travel writer. My work is to appraise the worthiness of a meal, the firmness of a bed. I run my finger over the tops of dressers, I ask desk clerks to perform impossible tasks (to get me a car when there are none to be had, to provide a box lunch when the kitchen is closed) in order to see how accommodating they can be. Mine is not a job of conviction, but of details. Departure times, the costs of rooms, the distance between things.

Whatever I became involved in here, I want to tell him, has nothing to do with my feelings for the state, but everything to do with my feelings for a person. However, Major Lorenzo does not care about such things. He has come to inform me of my options—options that will produce more red tape. He leans forward as he speaks, his arms resting on his knees, though his gaze is out the door, toward the street. For a moment I look that way too as if someone we both know might walk in the door. I hear him explaining why he doesn't think he can send me to Jamaica. "It is not customary to send you to another place. What we normally do, our policy, is to return you to your point of origin."

"Yes, but if I provided the money, the cash . . . ," I offer.

"Well, that might help." I stare at him for a moment,

wondering when Major Lorenzo stopped looking me in the eye. I don't remember when he began glancing at sheets of paper, gazing at the floor, out into the plaza, and this reminds me of someone, not anyone very close, but someone who frightens me.

"Let me go make a phone call," I ask him. "Maybe I can clear this up . . ." I excuse myself and go to my room, where I place a collect call to my editor, Kurt, at Easy Rider, and, of course, as I assumed it would, this call goes right through. "Maggie," Kurt says, accepting the charges, "it's not the same around here without you." Kurt has been trying to get me in bed for years, though I think it's more like a dog chasing a car. What would the dog do with the car if he caught it?

Kurt, who is approaching fifty faster than he would like, started Easy Rider almost three decades ago. His first guidebooks were to Central America and Bali and he claims to have started it all—hippie travel, backpackers. The stick-out-your-thumb kind of travelers. He takes full responsibility for the Galápagos and ecotourism. Of course, his readers have grown up with him and now they have kids and thinning hair and they are less inclined to go where they can't eat the salad. Now we publish a survivor's guide to Disney World and a Europe with kids, which lists every safari park and water slide on the Continent, and Todd keeps threatening, once we've got a few more house payments under our belt, to go, though so far we haven't.

About once a year, for all the paying of my dues, Kurt hands me a plum. Jessica and I did Galápagos last year, where blue-footed boobies walked right up to her hand. Sardinia. A barge tour along the Danube. He sent us to Jamaica a few years ago, where it rained the whole time and Todd kept staring out the window, looking for the sun. Go with the flow, I told him. I didn't mind being inside, curled in damp sheets with paperback novels, watching Errol Flynn on TV. Now I'll tell Kurt he owes me one. A four-star restaurant tour of France, the Dolomites. "What's wrong, Maggie?"

"What's wrong is that I'm in some kind of trouble and I want you to guarantee me a ticket to anywhere."

"Are you serious about this?" he asks.

"Kurt," I tell him, "I am completely serious."

"Then I'll do what I can."

I gaze around my room. It feels small, sterile. Cobwebs have appeared in a corner. "You have to do better than that," I tell him. "You need to promise that you'll get me out of here."

"Maggie, there are no foreign journalists in jail there."

But I am not being kept here as a journalist. I am being punished by someone in a rage. That is what is starting to become clear to me. An enraged man whose daughter has denounced him, that's what is keeping me here. When I hang up, I find that I am shaking, as if someone had just walked in and startled me. My body shakes as I long for things that are far away. I miss Todd and I miss Jessica and I lie back on the bed and weep. My pillow, my dog, the room where I sleep. The sound of familiar footsteps in the hall. I miss talking on the phone and not wondering who is listening in. Am I supposed to tell someone something? Is there something they have to know before they'll let me leave?

But the truth is, I know nothing, except that Isabel is gone and perhaps I helped her depart. Perhaps I did not. I know nothing of what happened or became of her after the last night I saw her, though, of course, this was our plan.

I press my face into the pillow and try to smell who has

been there before. I sniff for a scent of perfume, oil, the odors of human intimacy. But there is nothing there, not a trace. I sit up, thinking that I am supposed to confess. That when I go downstairs and see Major Lorenzo, I'll tell him all I know. A confession, that is what they want out of me. I'll tell him and he'll let me go.

Somehow relieved with my decision, I splash water on my face and go back downstairs. Major Lorenzo and his aide are still sitting on the wicker settee in the lobby. I decide that I will go up to Major Lorenzo now and tell him all my secrets, whatever it is he thinks I know. That she's hiding in Jamaica, that she's living in Madrid, that she never left *la isla*. That I could love my family more and my intrigues less, that my restlessness is the source of all this trouble, but I am not an enemy of the state. I am prepared to say this and more. It has only been three days, but I can easily imagine the defeat of the coerced confession, the empty hole that true confinement must be.

As I walk toward Major Lorenzo with Isabel's name on the tip of my tongue, I notice Manuel sitting at the bar. He seems to have this sixth sense about me, about when I'll show up. Or perhaps he is just always here. I think I see Major Lorenzo and Manuel exchanging glances, but I cannot be sure. But there is something about Manuel's presence that fortifies me. I feel a seismic shift. I know nothing; there is nothing to tell. The matter has all been misconstrued and the essential thing is for me to leave.

I go up to Major Lorenzo and inform him that I have spoken with my boss and he has guaranteed me a plane ticket anywhere out of here and Major Lorenzo nods. "So," he says, "we'll see what we can do."

"Have you been to Jamaica?" I ask him.

"Yes," he says, getting up to leave, "it is a lovely place."
Then he looks at me rather coldly. "But we have very nice
beaches here."

After he walks out the door, Manuel motions for me to
join him at the bar. "I've been thinking about your calling
Rosalba, because perhaps she could help you," he says after
our coffees arrive. "But I don't think it is a good idea. In fact,
it is a bad idea. But I have some friends and they are trying to
see if we can't get this matter cleared up."

"I'd just like to get out of here as soon as possible."

Manuel nods. "Of course, that would be best."

"I'm thinking I should tell them everything. I should tell
them what I did, about helping Isabel."

Manuel looks at me sternly. For the first time I think he is
angry with me. "That is a very bad idea. Don't even think
about that again."

After a pause, I glance up at him. "Do you hear from
Isabel?" I ask. "Does she write to you?" I had not wanted to
ask him this question because I'd never heard from her myself
and I didn't want to know, but now suddenly I do.

"Isabel is fine. Her daughter is with her now."

"You mean he let Milagro go."

Manuel nods again. "Oh, yes, he let her go."

Nineteen

I'VE ALWAYS SLEPT in Mummy's bed, Milagro told me when I saw her again. I can hardly remember sleeping anywhere else, except on nights when it is very hot and we sleep outside under the *júcaro* tree. Mummy gathers those round little leaves to make our bed and the leaves smell sweet, like sap, and the air is full of the scent of the jasmine tree. Otherwise I sleep curled in her bed, but I like it best sleeping in the garden because inside Mummy wraps me tight and holds me until I can hardly breathe.

She opens the windows wide so the breeze blows in, what little breeze there is, but I wake up hot, sweaty, trapped in her arms. Even when she's married or when a man lives with us, I sleep with her and he sleeps in the room that was mine. Only the last husband seemed to mind and this is probably why he went back to Caracas.

Sometimes Mummy goes away. She'll be gone for a night or a week, and then I go upstairs and stay with Rosalba. But I never sleep well alone in her closed rooms, in the narrow beds.

Mummy lets men break her heart. I've watched this over and over again. Of course, El Caballo was the first one to break her heart. I cannot tell you how many times she told me about the night he came and danced with her. How she still waits for him to come and take her away. Really, it was as if nothing important ever happened to her, before or since. I think she's just been waiting for him, all these years, the way you wait for a bus that's not going to come.

In the meantime she falls in love with all kinds of guys for a week. A month, a day. She'll spend a weekend with one; a year with another. Once she fell in love with the man who painted our house. They became lovers while he was painting it yellow. And when he was done, she said she wanted it blue like the sky on a clear day. He said no and that was the end of that. It's always the same. She'll tell me, Milie—that's what she calls me, Milie—I've met the one. For me there can be no other. And then six months later she won't remember his name.

The ones she usually meets come from other places. They have a mother who's Mexican or they are here on business. Once she spent a few months with a Russian engineer who was working in agronomy. He was the most boring man you could imagine. All he talked about was bushels per acre and irrigation systems, but she'd say, I'll marry him, Milie, and he'll get us out of here. But of course he never did. None of them ever will. They just come and go.

Mummy is crazy. I have to say that. She is crazy. But I don't care. It's not bad crazy. She decorates the house in flower petals and the pictures of the saints. She dresses all in white so she looks like a ghost, like somebody carved her out of marble, and goes to the house of Ángel, the *santero*, where they sacrifice goats and drink blood. Rosalba screams at her that Ángel puts things in people's heads. That what kind of a jerk drops sixteen palm-tree seeds into a tray and from this predicts the future.

It's a bunch of crap, Rosalba says. Rosalba screams at her, Why don't you do something useful with your life. Do something for the revolution.

And Mummy says, Fuck the revolution; it's not my revolution. It's your stupid revolution. And Rosalba puts her hands over her ears, shaking her head.

Rosalba has tried to get Mummy jobs. Once they sent her off to pick tobacco for two weeks and I slept upstairs in the narrow bed. When she returned, her hands were all cut, scratched raw. I dipped them in egg white and wrapped them in torn sheets. Mummy says, My father is a tyrant and this country is run by tyranny.

Rosalba rings her hands and weeps. You don't know him, she says. He is a great man. You don't understand what we fought for.

He is a *pendejo*, Mummy replies, and I'm afraid I do understand.

My father lives in the center of town and I see him every day. He's an artisan and makes ceramics in a little shop. He comes over or I take a bus to his place. He makes me a cup of tea or we have a soda together. Sometimes he will scramble an egg, but mostly he gives his rations to us. His parents named him Ernesto, after Che. Do you have any idea how many people here are named Ernesto? He only lived with my mother for a few months after I was born. Mummy really doesn't want a man around the house. She says she doesn't like their smell and they take up too much room.

I don't always go to school. I don't go because there are often no buses to take me and once I arrive there are usually no pencils or books or teachers, for that matter. I don't like what I learn. About how to be a good revolutionary and serve the state. How to put government before personal goals. The history of *la isla* is a history of throwing off the yoke of oppression. And the kids tease me. They say I bet you have enough chickens to eat. You have enough eggs. It is true that we aren't starving, but we aren't exactly well-fed. I've never seen a lobster except in the sea.

I saw my grandfather once. He came to address my kindergarten class. He said he didn't want to bore us with a long speech, but we said, Oh no, *líder,* you won't bore us. So he talked for three hours about dialectics and his enemies and what we can do for the revolution, and we made paper airplanes and slept. Afterward when the teacher introduced me to him, he tapped me on the head like he wanted to hear if there was something in there.

When I don't go to school, I go down to the sea. This is where we like to hang out, my friends and me. My friends all have nicknames like El Gordo and Chichi. Chico is my boyfriend and we hang out on the seawall and do things. A lot of my friends go into the park at night and two of them had babies last year. But I just let Chico stick his hand in my blouse while we get wet from the ocean spray. Mostly we sit and think about all the things we want to have. It's like we're making our list for Santa Claus. I want Rollerblades and a CD player and a trip to Disney World. I like to chew gum and smoke Marlboros and draw pictures of the sea. But if somebody asks me what I want to be when I grow up, I say I want to be somewhere else.

Mummy wants me to have everything. I want to give you

the world, she says. Then she weeps because I don't even go to school. Everybody here just hangs out because there's nothing to do. Who cares about things, I tell her, I just want you to be happy. Mummy is so thin that when I hold her I think she will break in my arms. It is like hugging a bag of bones.

Rosalba screams at her. You don't eat and you don't do anything. So many nights I wake and feel Mummy's tears running down my neck. I want Mummy to go. Even if I have to sleep alone on the little cot in Rosalba's apartment, I want her to go because I know that if she goes, then I will follow. It may take a while but Mummy will find a way to get me out of here.

And then maybe I'll get to sleep in my own bed in a house with her. Maybe I'll be able to breathe again.

Twenty

BANANA TREES, stripped of their fruit, lined the Carretera Nacional. In the median strip, bushes of primrose bloomed. We were the only car on the highway, except for the pickup trucks carrying workers to and from the fields where they picked the oranges that never found their way into the stores. Because there was no traffic, the highway was ours. Isabel had bartered some extra gas rations and I brought the picnic—cheese, Spam, crackers, dried fruit. What was available at the tourist *tienda*.

She had been coming to my hotel, saying there were things she wanted to show me. For Easy Rider Guides I had a tight schedule, a carefully planned itinerary of things to do. There were walks I needed to take each day, restaurants where food needed sampling. There were seventeen colonial churches in Puerto Angélico alone that I was supposed to visit. But Isabel told me there were little villages tucked away where no one ever went, and cigar factories miles from any town. "If you want to know how this country works," she said with a laugh, "you should see the cane-processing plants." And I knew we were going to the beach.

We drove for an hour before we ran out of gas. Isabel banged on the gas meter, which read full. Damn, she said. It was blazing hot as we pulled off to the side of the road. We'll never get out of here, I thought. But it wasn't long before a car pulled up. A man in a blue polo shirt and polyester pants asked if he could help. He offered to siphon gas out of his car to get us to the station, which was about ten miles' drive. I was impressed with the generosity of this stranger in a country so short of gas, but Isabel took the gas without saying a word.

In the car she was silent, morose all the way to the gas station, for which there were no signs. "It's his job to follow me," she said. "You see, my father likes to know my every move. He monitors me, though, of course, he never sees me. Isn't that unbelievable?"

"I know it's not the same," I told her, "but my father used to make us stay home too . . . for the slightest thing."

She gave me a smile from the corner of her mouth. "So," she said, "then perhaps you know what I mean."

We drove to a secluded beach where mongooses overran the remains of a beach bar and the disintegrating thatch huts that lined the beach. Beneath one of the huts, Isabel spread out our blanket and picnic. Along the beach were makeshift love hotels—blankets and tents beneath which pairs of feet protruded. In the water perhaps a quarter of a mile out to sea couples stood in timeless embraces, bikini bottoms floating close beside them in the tranquil Caribbean Sea.

"I know all the secret places on *la isla*," Isabel said as she kicked off her sandals. "This is Playa de Paraíso. Only lovers come here. They can't afford hotels. I've been here myself a few other times." She gave me a wink. "Anyway, no one will bother us here. I love this beach. I've swam with the dolphins right where the waves break. I've found black and salmon-colored coral. Priceless shells. I keep them in a box in my room." She stripped down to her faded green bathing suit. "I loved a boy once," she said, watching the blankets that lined the beach move up and down, gazing at the lovers who stood like aquatic birds along the shore. "And we used to come here."

When I was twenty, I fell in love, Isabel said, stretching out under the thatched hut in the sand. He was the first man I ever loved and perhaps the only one. He was a student of law, just a few years older than me, and we decided to marry. We met in a café where we were both reading the same book. Lorca. So we had coffee together and started having coffee almost every day. We became great friends.

First, you know, it is important to be friends. There was so much we liked to do together. We both liked to swim. He was a wonderful swimmer and he could just stay in the water all day like a fish. And he loved to read and cook. I never ate much but I ate whatever he made. He cooked all kinds of food. He made *arroz con pollo, ropa vieja*. I had an appetite then. He lived in a little flat off the Miramar and we'd stay inside—played house, really. We'd read and write poems and compose love songs to each other. We kissed and lay in bed until it was time for me to go home to my mother.

It is difficult to believe, I know, but I was a virgin on my wedding night. We wanted to wait. We thought it should happen after we'd made our vows. That's how foolish we were. It's hard to believe now. He was very gentle when he made love to me. He never hurt me, not once. We lived together as a married couple for two weeks. It was the only happy time I've known.

I convinced my father to throw me a wedding. I had not been alone with my father since the night he came and danced with me and I hadn't heard from him since the day he tried to adopt me. We'd barely spoken in years, but he was always cordial when I saw him at official functions. So I went to his office one day and waited several hours until he would see me. He glared when I came in, but I just said, Look, I'm your only daughter and I am in love so I want you to give me a wedding. He hemmed and hawed, but in the end he agreed.

My father had the wedding at his hunting estate in the woods about twenty miles from the city. You know, he lives in many places, though he claims he only lives in a room in the apartment of his *compañera*, where he has a single bed and a balcony with a stationary bicycle. Every day people see him on that balcony, exercising fanatically, lifting weights, riding the bicycle.

While my father has no true home, he has many houses. There is a mansion on Eighty-third Street in Ciudad del Caballo and another in the eastern provinces where he also keeps a sugarcane *finca*. He is said to preside over its harvest. There is a fishing hut at Playa Negrita and a huge waterfront home on Isla Azul. There's his hunting estate, which he seized from an old aristocratic family. First he imprisoned the owner of the estate, though the man begged on his knees to be allowed to leave with his family. The family left but the man stayed in prison, where he died. When my father hunts, he has the air force strafe the mangroves to flush out the pheasants and quail that, of course, are raised on the property. Many pilots have crashed during this mission.

My father has a tiny island, called Cayo Doloroso, with swimming pools and bowling alleys that he saves for his special trysts with the dancers he imports from the various clubs and for special meetings with heads of state or foreign military advisers or drug lords. The island has an airport where people can be flown in under absolute secrecy. Here there are no visas, no passports. He can conduct his business in total isolation.

I have never been to any of these houses, except his office in the city and the hunting estate where my wedding was held. Most of what I know about my father is what I've heard, what has been told to me, but I do not doubt a word.

Often he reserves different houses for different women. I have heard that I have sixteen brothers, but I am said to be the only girl. They don't call him the Horse for nothing. There was the dancer at the Club Tropical and the mysterious blue-haired woman from Argentina. There was the woman who was just herself a child and the one driven mad by grief. The jealous woman, if you can imagine such a person with El Caballo, and even the American woman. And then there was the beautiful woman—my mother, of course. And the wife he trusted and the mistress who betrayed him. And the one who he can never forget because she told him the truth. But then she died.

He kept them all in different houses, where they raised their different children. One had the swimming pool shaped like a crocodile and the other had six white horses that she rode naked and the third killed herself in a tub of white rum and the fourth lives in a house of decay and twisted vines, wrapped in the past and a passion greater than any grief, longing for a body that a lifetime ago pulled away. When she sleeps, it is beside him; when she dreams, it is of him. At night I have heard her awaken at the sound of a car turning around at the end of our street. I have heard her whispering through the darkened rooms, as she listens for footsteps that have eluded her these past twenty-five years. *Mi Amor*, she says, is that you?

But he gave me a wedding where waiters in black jackets carried trays of jumbo shrimp on the tips of their fingers. Champagne was uncorked by the case. There were delicacies from the sea, drinks from coconuts and brandied fruit, colored umbrellas and santería costumes, salsa bands and disco bands played on different parts of the lawn, and of course the rum flowed, endless bottles of white rum. Lambs and pigs roasted on the spits, chickens sizzled on the grills.

My father will not eat in public. And he will not eat sitting down. He will not be photographed eating. But on this night he ate right beside me. He toasted me and my groom. And then when the music began, my father danced with me. It was an old Latin love song, "Bésame, Bésame," and I was embarrassed to be dancing to that song with my father. I should have been dancing with my husband, but anyway I danced with him in a way that I hadn't danced since I was eight years old and had felt like a broom, sweeping the floor clean.

Two weeks after the wedding, my husband was drafted into the army and sent to fight a foreign war. Once more I went to my father's office, and this time I begged him not to send my husband. I pleaded, but he said it was not his jurisdiction; he said there was nothing he could do. You are the head of the armed forces, I shouted at him. How could this not be your jurisdiction? My husband was a slight, studious man. He collected cowrie shells that he made into a necklace for me before he left. And, of course, he never returned.

□ □ □ □

The first time we came to the beach I did not look at Isabel as she lay beside me in the sand, but now I did. I stared at her green suit, worn thin. In places I could see through to her skin. Her bronzed legs were riddled with blue lines. Her long, skinny arms drooped at her sides and she reminded me of a marionette, resting on its strings. But suddenly she stood up and turned and dashed down to the water and dove in. She splashed and I ran after her.

The water was warm and the sand soft as a mattress underfoot. It was shallow for almost a half mile out to sea and Isabel swam in that clear water. She swam straight out for a long time, then back again. "Come with me," she said, "I want to take you somewhere."

She led me toward the edge of the bay, where the shoreline curved just beyond some rocks. It was easy to walk on the soft sand, which felt warm between my toes. Where the shoreline curved, Isabel climbed onto a rock and pointed to a small island on the other side of the bend, not more than two hundred yards from where we were. "That is Redondo," she said, "the round island. The island is like a doughnut and in the middle there is a little beach, called Playa de Amor. When the tide is low, we can reach that beach. Can you swim that far?"

"Yes, I think I can."

Isabel took me by the hand and together we jumped off the rock into colder, rougher seas, unprotected by the bay. She swam first, pulling me along, then when she was sure I could swim in the rougher water she swam beside me. I could see her sleek legs as they kicked, her face so intent as she turned to breathe. Soon we reached the round rock and Isabel motioned for me to follow her. We swam around to the far side where seabirds nested, gulls and gull-like birds with blue feet, others with red, as if they were wearing plastic gloves. Brown pelicans cruised overhead.

Around the side of the island we came to a narrow channel that the sea had cut through the rock. Down that channel, which was perhaps just a hundred feet long, I could see a circle of turquoise water and a white beach, surrounded by rose-colored rock. Isabel pointed the way and said, "We have to swim through here, but just let the current carry you. Don't fight it when the waves pull you back." Water battered the sides of the narrow channel and I was afraid of being smashed against the sides, but I let the sea carry me. Soon we were tossed like flotsam onto that crescent of white sand where, Isabel said as we flopped down, lovers and pirates and poets have come. We lay on our backs on this inland beach, a circle of blue above us, crisscrossed by seabirds. Orange and blue crabs crawled across the wall of rocks behind us. The sea had dug caverns into the rock, pounding like thunder. "For me," Isabel said with a laugh, "this is what I call never-never land. But then the tide comes in and I have to leave." I glanced at our narrow cavern, wondering how long we had.

Once again Isabel took off her halter, but this time I didn't look away. I stared at her round, firm breasts, pointed toward the sky. My breasts are large, pendulous. Melons, Todd jokes, fondling them. It was not that I wanted to caress hers or suck on them. I wanted to lay naked on my back in the sun. I thought how I could easily spend days here on remote beaches, eating shellfish and dried fruit. How I could lie beside Isabel and smell her sunscreen and her Nina Ricci and her soap and listen to her tell me about Portuguese sailors and snakes sleeping on her chest and a father who came one night and danced with her.

I turned to Isabel and said, "I was thinking that I could help you. Or that I want to help you. There must be something I can do?"

Isabel frowned, shaking her head. "I don't know. I doubt it."

"But when I get home, there must be something I could do for you."

"Oh, especially not then," Isabel said, thoughtfully. "There is something that could be done here, but there are risks. I could not ask you. No, I don't want anyone implicated in my life. I will just stay here and grow old and die and it will have been a stupid life."

Suddenly I felt as if I could not bear her suffering anymore. "But I want to help you. Tell me what it is."

She touched my cheek. "You are a beautiful woman. You have a family and a life and you will go home and forget all about this. You will forget all about me. It will be as if none of it ever happened to you."

"No, I won't. I'll never forget you."

She patted my face again and I felt rough sand against my skin. "Oh, yes, you will."

Then she closed her eyes and seemed to fall asleep. I watched her for a little while, then I must have dozed off too. Suddenly she was shaking me. "Now we must go. In another hour it will be impossible to leave."

The salty water stung my skin; my lips were cracked. When we got back to land, we realized how burned we were, but neither of us cared. We hardly spoke on the ride back to the city.

That night after she dropped me off, my skin burned and I could not sleep. I lay down on my bed, still feeling the sand, the sun on us. I thought of the deep sadness in her eyes. All night long, whenever I closed my eyes, I saw hers.

After that night I began to dream of Isabel. I saw her in the turquoise blue sea. She was swimming, waving to me. And then she turned, diving like a fish, and I watched her swim away.

Twenty-one

LATER Major Lorenzo returns and says that the people who spoke with me yesterday would like to speak with me again. It is just a formality, he says, while we are trying to clear this thing up. Again he laughs, makes his usual comments about red tape, but something about him is altered. "It is taking too long," I say.

"Oh," he assures me, "it's just a matter of a little time now."

First we drive toward the Miramar, which is not the way we went before, and then, just before reaching the sea, we veer to the right and head straight out of the city, along the old port with its rotting docks, ships that look as if they haven't sailed in years. It is a cloudy day and for a while I can catch glimpses of the sea until we turn off again, heading toward an industrial part of town that I did not even know existed.

Though I cannot say that I mind getting out of the hotel, it bothers me that we are not going the way we went before.

We are going to a different place so I try to memorize the route, thinking it might be useful, but everything looks the same. The buildings could be buildings anywhere. We pass a park with empty swings that I do not recall passing the other day. People line up for food around the block at a ration store. An old woman walks home, a chicken dangling from her fist.

I cannot determine if we are going east or west and Major Lorenzo is oddly silent, staring straight ahead, as if there is no longer any reason for politeness. He does not ask me if I want the window up or down, but rolls it down, all the way, his arm resting on the door. The wind blows my hair straight back like when a dog sticks his head out the window of a moving car. We drive past the Plaza of the Heroes of the Revolution where the giant statue of a worker stands, and now I am certain we are going a different way and we are going to a different place.

Details that did not matter before seem critical now. What are the three things ocean navigators require to set their course: the celestial bodies, the wind, ocean swells. But the sky is cloudy and I cannot see the sun. The wind would be blowing off the sea. And I cannot read the ocean swells. No buildings look familiar, but the billboards all look the same. The smiling worker in the sugarcane field, the circle of tobacco rollers working together. There are no more distinguishing landmarks and I cannot get my bearings.

We are leaving the city by a highway and from what I can determine we are heading northwest. Once again wild primrose grows on the median strip. Along the road, sugarcane workers wave, and some try to hitch a ride. Major Lorenzo waves back, but signals no, his hand twisted up into an apology. They see his olive green shirt, the bars on his sleeve. Some salute and he gives little salutes back.

The sun is warm on my face and I close my eyes, thinking that this will all be over soon, and yet it seems as if there is nothing but time. The road has few cars, but many people are walking, and most hold out a thumb when they see us. A woman in a pink dress with gold earrings tries to hitch a ride. This time Major Lorenzo smiles and shrugs. He and his aide share a glance and laugh. I know if I weren't in the backseat they would give her a ride.

At last we come to a road that we follow to a small town. In the town all the houses are cinder-block and it doesn't exactly feel like a town. There is barbed wire and a kind of fence around it and soldiers seem to be everywhere. I realize we have come to some kind of a barracks. Some official place. We pull up in front of a simple cinder-block building with few windows and no door and both Major Lorenzo and his aide leap out and quickly lead me inside.

Inside the dark, cool building, a soldier is waiting at the door. "Thank you," he says to Major Lorenzo and asks me to follow him. I turn to Major Lorenzo, who nods. "It's all right, Maggie," he says. "We will be right here."

I panic at the thought of being separated from Major Lorenzo, who gives me a small salute as he gave the people who lined the road. "Please," I ask, surprised to hear my own voice, "can't you come with me?" He shakes his head and makes a motion with his hand to follow the soldier who is waiting for me at the door of a room.

In the stark room with just a desk and three chairs, a man in uniform sits at a desk. He has more bars on his sleeve than Major Lorenzo does, so I assume this is his superior. Next to the man sits the overweight man who spoke with me before.

He is dressed in the same civilian clothes he wore the other day—a blue guayabera that has crescent-shaped sweat circles under the arms—and the air is heavy with the smell of sweat. Neither man rises or shakes my hand, but the man in the uniform motions for me to sit down.

"Miss Conover," he begins, "we are hoping that you will cooperate with us. We seem to have a puzzle here, some pieces of which are missing, and we are hoping you will provide what we need. We have some things we would like to ask you and after we ask you these things—if we are satisfied with the answers—you may go. That is, you may return. We are as anxious as you are to finish with this matter and send you home."

Tears well up in my eyes. "Yes," I say, "I am ready to go home." I bite my lips, fight the tears. I do not want them to see me cry. I feel prickly sweat break out on my skin and I am trembling. I don't want them to see me sweat. I breathe deeply, but it doesn't seem to work.

"Good, then we both want the same thing and that is very important, isn't it?"

"Yes, that is very important."

"Could you please tell us who you work for?"

"I work for Easy Rider Guides."

"And what is the nature of your work?"

I answer questions I have heard before by rote. "I do updates. I visit places, hotels, restaurants. I write about them." Something in the way he asks these questions makes me feel he is trying to bore me, make me feel sleepy. Put me off-guard.

"And do you always befriend people when you travel?"

"I meet people when I travel."

"And whom did you meet when you were last here?"

"I don't remember. No one in particular."

"We have reason to believe," he said, leaning forward into his hands, "that you became friendly with Isabel Calderón when you visited *la isla* two years ago. Is that correct?"

I try to think of a way out of this direct question and I cannot find one, but I am thinking that if I just answer the question then we can get on to something else and I can begin to think about going home. "Yes, that is correct." I close my eyes as I answer. Friendship cannot be a crime even here. "I met her and we became friendly."

"And so," the fat man says, "you lied to us before."

I am trying to decide if I should respond to this, but the man in uniform ignores what he says. "And how would you categorize that friendship?"

I shrug. "We did some things together. She took me to the beach."

He and the fat man exchange glances as if they think that at last they are getting somewhere. And I suppose that in some sense they are, but I wish they weren't. I am trying to stay one step ahead of them. To give them what they want so as not to annoy them and yet not give them so much that it will create a problem for me.

"And did you not in some way try to assist Ms. Calderón in leaving *la isla*?"

I take a deep breath and wish now more than anything that I had listened to Lydia and never come back. "No, I did not assist her."

The uniformed man sighs. "Miss Conover, it is better if you tell us the truth, because we can only let you go when you do. Now let me ask you again: Did you in any way assist Miss Calderón in leaving *la isla*?"

"I think I would like to see a lawyer. Or someone from an embassy."

"Yes, of course you would, but that will have to wait until later. At any rate, this is only an informal inquiry."

"But I believe I have the right . . ."

He waves his hand as if he is swatting at some insect in the air. "Miss Conover, I would like you to answer the question."

"I am sorry but I don't know if I assisted Isabel Calderón in leaving this country."

"Did you report your passport and plane ticket missing the last time you were here?"

"Yes, they were lost. Or perhaps they were taken from me."

"And how were they lost? Or taken from you?"

"I don't know. I went to get them from my bag the day before I was to leave and they were gone."

The two men glance at each other and the man in uniform has a look of disdain on his face. He looks down at his watch, and then at me as if I am keeping him from somewhere else he has to be. I have no watch and no sense of what time it is, but there is a hollow feeling in the pit of my stomach and I sense that it is lunchtime. My head is starting to ache and I think I must be hungry.

"We will take a short break now," the overweight man says. "You might need some time to think." The two men suddenly get up and say they will return in half an hour. A guard is told to escort me to the bathroom if I wish and get me something to drink. I am taken down a corridor, where the bathroom consists of a cement cell and a seatless toilet. I squat, only to realize that once again there is no toilet paper.

I return to the room, feeling soiled, and the guard brings

me an orange drink. It is warm, but I am thirsty so I sip it slowly. I'm not sure how long I wait before the two men return with sated looks on their faces, as if they have just eaten well.

"Miss Conover," the uniformed man begins again, "Isabel Calderón is a pathetic creature who preys on the sympathies of others. She uses people in this way. We hope you did not allow yourself to become involved with such an unfortunate person."

"I don't see how . . ."

"She cannot get along with her father so she makes a spectacle out of herself and calls that politics. That is pathetic, wouldn't you agree?"

I am thinking about food—shrimp, fruit salad, bread. These are the thoughts that swirl through my mind. What I would order for lunch. They have eaten and they want me to know this. They want me to be hungry.

"I wouldn't know, sir."

"You see," the fat man breaks in as he lights a cigarette, "we have no desire to detain you or impede you. In fact, it is not in our interests to do so. On the other hand, we cannot have our laws ignored . . ." The uniformed man glances at the fat man.

"Miss Conover," the uniformed man says, "can you tell us where Miss Calderón is now?"

"I cannot. We have not been in touch."

"She has not written to you or tried to contact you?" At last after two years I am grateful to Isabel because I do not have to lie. She has protected me so that at this moment I would be able to say the truth.

"I have not heard a word from her."

"We have reason to believe that you are on *la isla* under false pretenses."

"I'm afraid I don't understand, sir."

This time the two men stare straight at me. The fat man shrugs, then sighs. "Mrs. Conover," the uniformed man begins again, "who are you working for?"

"I've already told you."

"Perhaps you could tell us again."

Twenty-two

I PICTURE Isabel living in a small town on the Costa del Sol. A town bleached white, stucco houses with blue trim. She rents two rooms that look toward the sea and she opens the windows wide, takes a deep breath. The widow who owns the house only wears black and Isabel can see her climbing the cobble-stoned hill from the market. In the morning the widow brings Isabel fresh bread, a steaming bowl of coffee laced with milk. Slowly, sleepily Isabel begins her day.

Perhaps the memoir she is writing begins like this: *When I was born, he canceled Christmas. It was the first holiday to go. He canceled Easter when I was three, but I remember dipping eggs in colored dye, searching for them at the base of the tamarind tree, in the curves of the screw pine. But Christmas I have never known. Never seen the bright strings of lights, packages tied in silver bows, never tasted pudding. Only my grandmother knew how to make salted cod stew and her recipes died with her.*

As Isabel sits at her wooden desk writing, she gazes out to

sea. It is not the same sea she remembers, but it will have to do. It is a sea she can live with. In the late morning she walks down to the shore. She goes there to think, to put her feet in the water. When she does this, she thinks that the water her feet touch reaches the shores where her mother still lives. This gives her some small consolation, the strength to go on. She likes the feeling of cold waves through her legs, her toes sinking in wet sand.

In the afternoon she takes her manuscript to a café, where she reads over what she has written that day. She glances at the dedication page and ponders how she has dedicated this book to the gringa who helped her get away. And also to those who have stayed behind. She pauses, looking up at the blinding-white town, the brilliant afternoon sun, so similar to the liquid light with which she was raised. She thinks she should write to the gringa, but she does not. She believes it is better this way. To cut the ties, not to implicate anyone.

Twenty-three

WHEN MAJOR LORENZO drops me back at the hotel, I try to phone home, but the operator tells me the circuits are busy; I cannot get through. I ask her to keep trying, but she says she doubts she'll be able to get through for several hours. Perhaps not until tomorrow, she says. I begin crying uncontrollably. I weep alone in my room because I know that the circuits aren't busy. They have just decided not to let me get through, just as they will decide when they want to let me go. I am a captive as surely as if I were in a cell.

I have often wondered, since I travel so much, what it would be like to be on an airplane that is about to crash and to realize that you will not see certain people you love again. Do you think about the last time you touched that person, the kiss good-bye, the way your child's hand felt in yours? Or is it the future that will possess you at that moment—how will my child live without her mother? How long will they grieve? What are the millions of little ways in which we need one another? I can see Todd, trying to find an object he knows I would be able to find, suddenly knowing what it is to miss me.

Someone has decided that for now I will not be able to get my calls through. That I will not hear the voices that perhaps keep me going more than I can know. Maybe this is the way they have chosen to make me crack. To let me sink into the great gray void that comes upon a person who has been lost or abandoned, who can no longer find the way home. But they will not break me because I know they cannot keep me forever and that eventually they will let me go.

Unless, as Manuel has suggested, they decide I am some kind of a spy. But that seems so far-fetched that I push the thought away. I will keep busy, I tell myself. Occupied. That is what will get me out of here. But splashing cold water on my face, I wonder how I will make it through.

The people at the hotel are getting to know me. I have only been here three days, but already they seem to be accustomed to my routines. The maids wait until I tell them they can clean my room. The waiters know how I like my coffee, at which table I prefer to sit. I like the one at the entrance, near the wrought-iron grating. Through the grating, which is really black bars, I can look into the lobby and see who is coming and going.

There are definitely regulars who frequent this place. There are certain groups of women, pretty, who attach themselves to male tourists of an Aryan nature. Two men in white suits are in the lobby every morning. I can watch them from my table through the grating, but now it occurs to me that they can also watch me. I am not so unlike the monkey in the zoo. I don't think of myself as a prisoner yet, though clearly I am one.

As I sip my afternoon coffee, the prostitutes arrive. They seem to live in this lobby, but now they flock to my table, pulling up chairs. "Hey," says Eva, with her red lipstick and short skirt, "we've seen you around the hotel for a few days now." She looks at me more closely, staring into my red eyes. "You got a cold or something?"

They must be worried that I'm cutting into their trade. "Yes, I've got a cold," I tell them. They nod, concerned, and I wonder if I look sick. "And I'm allergic," I go on. "To the sun. I get spots."

This time they laugh. "Like a leopard," Flora says.

"Maybe you should go out at night," Eva says with a coy laugh. "We'll take you out for a good time some night. You can avoid the sun."

"Hey that's a great idea," María says. "You can go out with us."

"Why not?" I tell them, my spirits suddenly buoyed by this idea. I imagine myself in dark glasses, red lipstick, a rose-pattern spandex jumpsuit around my rounded hips and ample breasts.

"Yes, you could come out with us," María says. "We'll show you a good time. We'll go dancing." She stands up and starts to dance, shaking her hips furiously. Flora looks at her with a mix of amusement and indifference. Eva claps along. A group of young Dutchmen stands at the bar and they too begin to clap. Soon Flora drifts over to their table. Business is starting to brew, so Eva and María join her and I am left alone.

A few years ago I wrote a weekly column for a travel magazine and after a while it seemed that either no one read those columns or my readers had no idea about the places I wrote about. So I began to write about places that do not exist. The Mulaganese Islands, for example, off the coast of North Africa, with their complex history of piracy and prisoners. Under Portuguese rule for four hundred years, and then British until modern times, the Mulaganese were renowned for the wool of their sheep and their strategic placement during half a millennium of colonial wars. Now they export sweaters and live on mutton stew.

I wrote of other places: the Perdido Islands, off the coast of East Africa, with their practicing cannibals and beaches, huge stelae over three stories high and carvings equal only to Easter Island's, written in a language believed to be related to ancient Polynesian. I wrote of Daridnea, a small country near Argentina, inhabited with tiny monkeys and the giant two-toed sloth. And Straccatelli, the only remaining Italian city-state whose inhabitants live as they had seven hundred years ago, in stone huts, still painting frescoes of martyred saints on their walls.

I found I did better with places that didn't exist, and I wrote about them well. Kurt was amused, but too many readers complained, saying they had been unable to make bookings or find tours to take them to these remote isles and solitary countries. I had warned my readers that if they wanted to see these places, they needed to go immediately. We live in a world that will soon have no uncharted terrain. No species to be discovered. No Stone Age peoples living at the end of a jungle path. The Straccatellis, as we know them, I wrote, in a few years will no longer exist.

La isla, of course, does exist. Don't let anyone fool you about that. It just feels as if it doesn't. But it does.

Twenty-four

SELECTED NOTES for the Guidebook:

Islands are apparent worlds.
—REINA MARÍA RODRÍGUEZ

The island was purgatory.
—VICTOR HERNÁNDEZ CRUZ

Island: a body of land surrounded by water.
—Webster's

Islanders are outsiders.
—ISABEL CALDERÓN

Twenty-five

THE CHURCH of the Apparitions was on a cul-de-sac near the waterfront. It was at this site that the Virgin had appeared to believers on innumerable occasions, her plaintive face etched into the swirls of an ancient ash tree around which the faithful built their church. Passions have been enacted. It was one of the most desired spots in the Americas for pilgrims and true believers. While not known for its architectural splendors—there was no vaulted ceiling, no impressive colonnades or faded frescoes—the church was a must-see on the tourist circuit and hence a part of my colonial churches walking tour.

But it was Isabel, of course, who told me to go there the first time I met her. And when she dropped me off after Playa Negrita, she told me again. "You must see it," she said. For years I have resisted the must-sees that the traveler is always faced with, because someone else's fond memory probably won't be my own. You might remember that great meal in the South of France or that wonderful Amazon guide, but it doesn't mean I will be able to experience that meal as you did or enjoy the sense of humor of your guide.

However, I do tend to listen to what the natives tell me to do and see, and Isabel told me twice to go to the Church of the Apparitions, so I decided I had to go. I found it with some difficulty on a quiet Friday morning after being sent down several wrong streets and dead ends. The people of *la isla* are famous for giving wrong directions. This is not malicious; they just want to appear helpful. When I arrived at the church it was almost noon.

Slipping into its cool darkness, for an instant I was blind and my eyes adjusted slowly. At the end of the aisle of the church, where the altar should be, the ash tree took shape, looking like something out of a Disney cartoon. Angry, swirling, rising from some child's punitive nightmare. I walked to the front of the church and touched its bark. Standing back, I saw many things in its swirls, but not the Holy Mother. Beside the tree people knelt, touching it. A man kissed the trunk as if it were a woman. A child caressed its bark.

Against the wall crutches had been cast aside, body braces shed like skin, prostheses were discarded as if their owners had sprouted new limbs. There were eye patches, slings, plaster casts, but mainly I was struck by the piles of crutches—in descending order by height, at the end of which stood those of the lame children who had hobbled away.

Miracles don't really appeal to me. They never have. I don't believe in prayers answered, faith restored. I don't expect that my mammogram will be fine because my work on earth isn't done. I don't think kindnesses will be returned in mysterious ways. I used to pray for things. Lydia and I prayed by the sides of our beds that our father wouldn't notice the light she'd left on in the garage or the dirty dish I'd left in the sink. We prayed that we could sneak downstairs and not get caught. That our mother would start working during the day. That we'd come home and find a pot roast on the stove.

Lydia still prays. She prays in an ashram upstate and she prays to a statue of the Virgin in Queens that cries real tears. She gets up at four A.M. to chant her prayers. Todd is the opposite. He believes that if he works hard he will prosper and if he takes care of himself he'll be fine. I think they're both fanatics. I think that when we're all together, I'm the only realist in the room. I'm not one of those people who gets on a plane and says this plane won't crash because I'm on it. I get on the plane and say I hope these mechanics aren't the scabs they hired during the strike last year.

I sank onto a pew, catching my breath. Sweat poured down my brow. Suddenly I found I wanted to pray. I too had been feeling lonely and bereft. I missed Jessica and wanted to go home. Every night I phoned and sang lullabies to ease her into sleep. Now a sense of despair came over me that I found difficult to explain. I walked with no crutches, no white cane, and yet I wanted something to cure me—of what I could not be sure.

The church was dark and a few old women muttered on their knees. A nun begging for alms stopped by my pew and I gave her a few dollars. She said a blessing over me as she stumbled on. Then I walked to the back of the church, where there was a list of the sightings of the Virgin and the miracles performed. Pictures of sick children, ailing fathers, and dying mothers were pinned to the wall. Grief was palpable everywhere. Next to some of the photographs were short letters recounting miraculous cures, remissions, sudden reversals. The tumors that disappeared, the asthma that never recurred, the twisted limb made straight again, the eyes that could suddenly see.

The saints that lined the walls were white, skin pale as eggs. Before them veiled faces knelt. As I turned to leave, I noticed a woman from behind, staring into the face of a saint. She was thin and her dark hair fell to her shoulders. She was taller than many people there and even though I could not see her face, I knew that it was Isabel with her eyes fixed on the sad faces of the saints.

I sat back down on a pew and watched. Isabel stood motionless as a statue, hands twisted in front of her. Milagro, dressed in a Disney World T-shirt and chewing gum, leaned against the wall behind her mother. She stuck a note to the wall, then took her mother by the hand, and together they knelt as tears ran down Isabel's face.

In this room of crutches and canes, their hands encircled the tree. Milagro's eyes were just closed shut, as if she were sleeping, but Isabel's were clenched, her lips moving rapidly. She was praying for a miracle. She did not name her daughter Milagro for nothing, I thought as I slipped out of the church, back into the light of day.

I waited a few moments until they came out, Isabel leaning on Milagro's arm. Milagro seemed huge beside her frail mother, as if she could scoop Isabel into her arms and carry her down the street. I followed them as they walked through the narrow streets of the old city. Isabel kept her arm through Milagro's as they moved along.

They paused at a storefront I could not see and seemed to be admiring what was in the window. Perhaps a dress or a pair of shoes they wanted to buy. They laughed, tilting their heads as if to admire what was there. Then they walked ahead a few buildings and did the same thing. Admiring, then shaking their heads and walking on.

When I reached the shops where they paused, I looked inside. But the shops were empty. There was nothing there.

Twenty-six

I HAVE TAKEN to examining the objects in my room. Not the objects I have brought with me, though there are a few, but the ones the hotel provides for each visitor. The TV and its stand, the lamps, the minibar that does not refrigerate the little bottles of Coke and Fanta, the gray bottles of *agua mineral*. There had been a Snickers bar, perhaps left behind by a previous guest, but I ate it. There is a table and two wooden chairs that I move around to alter my view. Twin beds with a built-in nightstand between them so you can't push them together (you'll find this feature in Japan as well). The nightstand is equipped with knobs, which turn out to be for a radio. An old rotary phone. Three glass ashtrays. I am living in the Twilight Zone.

I have, however, brought certain things with me. A photo of Todd and Jessica in a canoe (a picture I always carry, though it is a few years old), my Scandinavian travel clock, the small stuffed bear Jess sticks in my suitcase for good luck. In my own house, I have few of these personal touches—no pictures on the wall. Our bedspreads are plaid, our sofas and chairs have rough, beige covers. It occurs to me as I spend hours in this room that I am able to make my hotel rooms homey and my home like a hotel.

On my desk at home I have one picture of my parents from before I was born. They are on a road, standing in front of an old car. He has his arm around her waist and they are laughing. I was born a year after this picture, and Lydia fourteen months later. I have no pictures of all of us together. In the evenings before my mother went to work, we sometimes all had dinner. My mother cooked on Sundays and froze whatever we'd need for the week. I'd open up the trunk freezer and find foil-wrapped packages with the days of the week written on them. We never knew what was inside until we defrosted them. After she died, my father still ate the meals she'd frozen for him for the next two years.

I liked staying home sick as a child because then my mother was home with me. I'd feel her cool hand on my head, the thermometer slipped between my lips. She brought me trays of hot soup, Jell-O, ice cream. Hospital food. Everything was hot and cold. All day my mother would check on me, and when it was time for her to go to sleep, usually in the middle of the afternoon, she'd lay down beside me and I'd watch her chest rising and falling.

I'm not sure when she moved into the guest room, but perhaps I was just fifteen. She never said a word about it. She just moved in her things. Eventually it was a room filled with mirrors, clocks, bottles of pills. She had shoe boxes all labeled with the same spelling error. High Heals, Low Heals. Time heels, I signed my notes to Lydia as we grew up.

My mother had a love of natural phenomena. In August we'd lie on lawn chairs all night long, watching meteorite showers. She taught me how to cross my fingers during a lunar eclipse so they made shadows shaped like crescent moons.

This hotel room is notable for what is missing. There is no Bible, no stationery, no phone book. There is only one object in my room that truly interests me. It is that frog, wedged between the wall and a slat of glass that forms a window in my bathroom. I have tried to pry open the window, but it won't budge. All night and all day long the frog sings.

It is always the same song. *Coquí, coquí.* The frog is saying its name. The coquí says its name because it is trying to make contact with its own kind. I really should ask someone in the hotel to unlock the window and let the frog go because it will starve if it stays where it is. But I have resisted so far because in a way this frog is the only company I have.

In the afternoon I nap, though it is difficult. I am used to sleeping with the door ajar. It is a mother's habit. All over the world, women are listening for a cry, a cough in the night. I have acquired this habit of listening.

I am awakened by noises, shouting in the street. And there is a crackling sound that I have heard in my own neighborhood in Brooklyn before. I run out onto the balcony to try and see. Then I hear footsteps, people running away. Is it a mugging? I wonder. Or some kind of unrest?

I get dressed and go downstairs, but the lobby is strangely quiet. No one seems to be around. I look and see that Enrique is not at his usual post. Finally I see him standing by the kitchen door. As I approach, he seems to avoid my gaze until I ask if he has heard anything, but he says no one has heard a thing. I ask him if it is possible that I heard gunfire. "It is possible," he tells me. "Anything is possible here."

Twenty-seven

I HAVE ONLY LIVED in houses of women, Rosalba told me when I went back again, looking for Isabel. Except for a few brief episodes, my life has been devoid of men. I grew up in rooms of petticoats and hand creams, tea cakes and curtains. My mother never remarried and we just lived together, my mother, Mercedes, and I.

There were a million things to do. My mother, an exacting businesswoman, tended the *finca*. I went to school. We had a housekeeper and Mercedes and money was not a problem. But there were no men in my life. So you can imagine how I felt the first time I saw him. I was no more than a girl when he came to help my mother balance her accounts. He wore a blue suit that was too small for him and carried a ledger book tucked under his arm. I would never see him in a suit again, or with a ledger book for that matter. They were burning the cane fields and there was the smell of dead things in the air. It made me sick, what I smelled that day, and the sky was filled with blackened smoke.

He never stopped talking. When he finished with his accounting for my mother, all he did was talk. The first time he came to me, he sat in the cane chair. And he began to talk about the peasants and how terrible it was that they had so little. He had traveled all across *la isla*, he had been to every village, and he saw things that he could not bear—children who died because there was no milk, young people gone blind.

And ignorance. He could not bear the ignorance. He said that it was by design that the people were not sent to school. He would make them go to school. He would create schools for them. And hospitals.

He talked about it for hours and hours, until my mother told him it was time for him to go home. I loved his voice as much as I loved anything about him, and, of course, I loved what he said. If a woman can be drawn to anything in a man, shouldn't it be to what he says? And then he went away, disappeared really, and no one knew for certain where he had gone, though rumors reached me that he had gone to work with the peasants in the fields.

Though a day did not go by when I did not think of him, it would be ten years before I saw him again. I married someone else, but when El Caballo returned to Puerto Angélico, the first thing he did was look for me. Of course, he was married at the time. He had married Clarita, the only wife he would publically acknowledge. They had gone to school together while he was studying law.

Clarita was a lovely girl with a gentle, kind face who could not know what misery was in store for her. I met her on several occasions at dinners, when she stood behind him, almost hidden behind his looming frame. She doted on him, but I cannot say that she really understood him. Her father ran a small grocery and her mother's family had some money from a farm they kept in the west. But of course they lost everything.

Clarita's mother had begged her not to marry him. That man will make you miserable, she said. I do not know this first-hand, but I have been told that she lived in a small, dingy apartment with no electricity or hot water and she waited for him while he was fighting in the hills.

But once he came back, once he saw me again, he could not stay away. Not that I wanted him to. There was no one else he could talk to the way he could talk to me. Clarita listened but with that blank stare of a woman who loves a man unconditionally, though she may not understand him. We scraped the money together to rent a tiny studio on the top floor of an apartment building near the Prado. I siphoned off money from my weekly allowance to pay for it.

It had an entrance off an alleyway, so it was easy for us to sneak in and not be seen. This was especially important for him because already he was getting well known. We furnished it with a simple bed, a small table, and two chairs, some dishes we found on the street. But I tried to make it nice. I brought yellow cotton sheets from home, sewed curtains out of an old floral fabric. I went to the *botánica* around the corner and bought votive candles, which we would burn in the light of the late afternoon. I bought statues of Santa Barbara and the Virgin Mother to protect us, and these I put over the mantel. When he came in, he kissed them first, then he kissed me, though no one would believe this if I told them.

At the *botánica* I also bought Desire Come bath oil and Nothing Can Go Wrong and Make Him Want Me floor washes. These, of course, I hid under the sink, where I knew he would never look. I always arrived before three o'clock and waited for him. While I waited, I bathed in the oils I'd bought, or scrubbed the floor on my hands and knees. I am not a superstitious woman, but for him I did these things. I arranged flowers, made tea. The things my housekeeper did at home.

Then I would lie upon the bed where the sunlight streamed in and listen for his boots on the stairs. Some days he would not come. Then I would leave, dejected, at five o'clock, returning to my life with my husband and Serena. Other days he would come and make fierce love to me for our two hours together, hardly saying a word. He would make love with a fury as if it were our last time together and often I feared it was. He is, as you know, a huge man and I am slight and sometimes he would hurt me, though I do not think he meant to.

There were times when he was preoccupied and just wanted to talk. Then I would pour glasses of iced tea and serve him little cakes, as if he had come for tea, and we would talk, but never about little things. He would not discuss his family or his personal life and he did not want to hear about mine. He wanted to talk about Tolstoy and Napoléon, about poverty and illiteracy. He made promises to me that he said he would keep for the whole country. If he won his revolution, he said, everyone would be able to read and have a place to live and work to do and food to eat. These are not small promises, but he made them to me and he kept them.

I loved his touch. There is no other way to say it. It wasn't that he was so skilled with women or knew how to touch them, it was more that he touched me in such an odd, tentative way. He'd lie on our bed, his hand just resting on my shoulder. Have you ever seen a child who wants to pet a dog but is afraid that the dog will bite? That is how he touched me. No one knows how vulnerable and afraid he is the way I do.

I think Clarita would have stayed with him if the letters had not gotten mixed up when he was in prison. You see, no one writes to his wife and mistress on the same day. That just shows how arrogant he was. He wrote to me and he wrote to Clarita. But he had his share of enemies and the letters were switched. I didn't mind getting her letter. I read how she was to enroll their son in the Jesuit school and how she was to handle the small amount of money that was left in the bank. He told her not to put the lights on at night and not to buy more than one chicken a week. He told her he wanted some books and an extra pillow.

But I can only imagine the letter she received. One in which he longed for my body to lie beside his. How his lips groped for mine in the nights, his hands reached for my breasts. How he lay awake at night, pretending I lay beside him.

That was the last straw for Clarita and she filed for divorce. Of course she lost her son. I don't think she would have anticipated that, but in the custody battle she lost him. It wasn't that El Jefe wanted his son; it was that he didn't want anyone else to have him.

One morning a few months after he was back from prison I woke and knew I was pregnant. It never even occurred to me that it could be Umberto Calderón's child because for years our lovemaking had been reduced to an obligatory Saturday-night intercourse, the raising of my nightgown to my waist, a quick, futile spurt that enabled him to sleep without the use of soporifics and rum with lime. My husband knew that it was not for him that I put on the almond creams and jasmine soaps, the oils scented with orange blossoms. It was for El Caballo that I put on the dresses of silk imported from China that lifted easily over my head. Though no matter how I scented myself, what permeated my flesh were the smells of his cigars, his rum.

I was a woman with Spanish eyes and aristocratic airs who lived in a house by the sea, whose cane furniture had been brought from Spain when *la isla* was still a colony, while El Caballo's great-grandparents toiled an inhospitable Galician soil. He had walked through my parent's house, filled with paintings of blue-eyed, fair-haired people who held their chins high, and this dark peasant had to have me. Everything about me, even my history, had to belong to him.

In that rented room in the late-afternoon light as we lay in bed, he told me that he saw a country where everyone had food and a roof over their head. Where children did not run naked through open sewers, but were in school all day long. He said, "Come with me, Rosa, and we will change the world."

I felt the child within me start to grow and I told Umberto Calderón that it was his. He nodded and seemed to accept it was so. He was a dour, dull man, the son of a local bureaucrat and a missionary. He was a decade older than I was and never comfortable with my fiery passions, my temperamental ways. Nor was he passionate, as I was, about the plight of the impoverished, the misery of their island. He just thought everybody needed to work harder.

One night I served Umberto *chicharrones de pollo* and *arroz con plátanos*, I served him *ropa vieja*. And then I gave him his coffee with cream and sugar. He stared at me in disbelief. "I have never eaten these things," he said. That night as he lay beside me, he said, "This is not my child."

I pleaded and tried to convince him that it was otherwise, but I knew it was useless. "I know whose child it is," he told me, "but I will accept it as my own, in name at any rate, as long as you do not humiliate me." It was not that I did not love Umberto. I did. I loved him the way you love anyone to whom you are indebted. I was patient and loyal, grateful that he paid the bills, gave me a home, and cared for me. But it was not a great love. It was not a passion.

When I told El Caballo about the child, he seemed happy. But when I told him I could not go with him, I could not join him in his struggle because of my children, he turned away from me. Slowly I watched him slip away. He could not forgive me for wanting my children more than I wanted his revolution. People have misunderstood him; history may not be kind to him. But he has always been true to what he believed. He never came to me again after Isabel was born, though I have waited for him all these years.

When Isabel was born, I could not bear the thought that I might lose this child, the way Clarita had lost hers. I convinced Umberto to recognize her. I promised him that I would stay with him and no one would know. So he gave Isabel his name, but never his heart. It was the best he could do.

Her birth came, as they often do here, during the great storm. It was hurricane season, and though the moon was full, the seas grew wild and the sky turned yellow. As the storm tore the island apart, I felt my daughter being born. My husband turned his back and would not take me to the hospital, so Mercedes drove as the wind blew us across the road. The sea pulled back, then roared again to the shore.

As wind struck, the mangrove forest that had lined the beach for a hundred years was twisted and ripped to shreds.

Toothpicks of trees remained and a strip of beach never seen from the apartment houses a half mile away was suddenly in clear view. The roof of the Sheraton was blown into a parking lot and a row of beach houses was leveled. The wall of a house across from ours was ripped off and one woman found a sofa belonging to someone else in her living room. When the waters receded a whale was found, bewildered and flailing, in a neighbor's pool.

In the hospital I labored in the dark to the sound of shattering glass. Patients screamed in terror as palm fronds crashed into their rooms. The child was upside down in my womb and the doctors could do nothing for me. I screamed in agony until Mercedes forced her way in, shoving aside an orderly and two nurses who were pinning me down, and she lay her trembling hands on my womb. Inside me, I felt the baby turn.

In the darkness my dark child was born, shiny and slippery as a fish. In her black eyes, I saw two stars, shimmering there. I do not know when it was that those stars went out, but I have looked for them over the years.

Twenty-eight

A MAID comes by my room and asks if I can do her a favor. "I have dollars," she whispers to me. She says she needs two pairs of shoes from the *tienda*. The natives are not allowed to have dollars and the *tienda* where the foreigners shop only takes hard currency. From behind her back she takes out a slip of paper; it is about four inches long. "I need a pair of red-and-black shoes this size; and another pair, two inches longer." She tells me that the woman in the *tienda* knows who she is and there won't be any problem.

The sight of this slip of paper four inches long moves me and I go to the *tienda* for her. After passing the jeans, the T-shirts, the straw hats, I find the shoes. There are children's sizes; tiny red-and-black shoes, white shoes, pink shoes. Little dresses. I run my fingers over them, touching them all. I try to imagine Jessica in a crinoline skirt, a ruffled blouse; socks with lace on the side. But she is a tomboy, given to sweat suits and jeans. Todd says studies show that tomboys make happier marriages, but I don't know.

It is late in the day and I miss her the most at this time. I decide to call her and say good night. I am the one who puts Jessica to bed. That's my job, but more than that, it is what I have to do. I don't remember anyone tucking me in, putting me to bed. I remember pulling back the covers and getting into bed. There was never a story or a song. I don't remember a bath or a book.

But with Jessica it's a whole ritual thing. The bath, the stories, the stuffed animals, the songs. It takes two hours and Todd says I am out of control. Excessive. He is often asleep when I patter into our room late at night. Before I left I made a tape of all the songs I sing to her. I wonder if she's been listening to the tape. But it's almost as if I am the one who can't sleep without the songs.

Just before I went on this trip, I lost my temper with Jessica. Todd had been working late and I must have been very tired. She wouldn't go to sleep and I couldn't get done anything I needed to. And then the dog sneaked into our room and peed on the bed. I screamed at Jessica that it was her fault and I never wanted a dog. I told her she was spoiled and never listened to what I said and if she didn't listen I'd give the dog away.

She screamed at me, "No, Mommy, no," and I had to go into my bedroom and shut the door. Afterward I knelt down at her bedside. I told her I wanted the dog and I didn't know why I shouted at her like that because I never had before.

I buy the shoes and take them upstairs to the maid. She clasps them to her chest, tears in her eyes, and thanks me profusely. Then I pick up the phone and try to call Jessica to say good night, but all the circuits are busy. I still cannot get a call through. Try back in an hour, the operator says, but in an hour Jessica will be asleep.

On the roof deck that evening Enrique appears. He orders a beer and sits down at a table across from me. I have been waiting for Manuel, but it seems that Manuel will not appear. Enrique smiles and asks how my visit is going and I tell him as well as can be expected.

Then he tells me, "You should be careful." He strokes his chin with his hand. "Be careful of where orders come from." He strokes his chin again and I understand that he is shaping his hand into a beard. "Don't trust," and he taps his hand to his shoulder. He does this two or three times, pointing to his shoulder, but I do not understand. Don't trust anyone, he tells me, slashing his finger under his chin. I can be arrested for telling you this, he says.

I stay on the roof deck a long time, hoping Manuel will show. After Enrique leaves, I order a daiquiri, which arrives the way I like it—bitter and frozen. Couples on the deck sit gloomily under floodlights; the music blares so loud that they cannot hear each other.

I go to the edge of the roof terrace and peer down. People are lined up to see a film; others are queued up for pizza. It is so peaceful and quiet down there; it is hard to believe that anything is wrong. There are lines in New York too, after all. For everything. There is a prison not far from the hotel, and through the prison's smoky glass I can almost see hands gripping bars. The shadows of men or women pace in their cells. Their crimes are petty thefts or perhaps writing on the wall the initials of the general who was executed a year ago on a drug charge no one believed.

I think that I would like to go downstairs and walk out of this hotel. To take a cool walk in the Ciudad del Caballo night, perhaps amble down to the sea, where lovers, or the lonely, or men who are on work rotation, sit. From the terrace I can see them, lining the seawall.

Twenty-nine

THE CLUB TROPICAL was located a few miles outside of town, in the outer reaches of the Miramar. It
was on an old estate, surrounded by palms that rose straight to
the sky. A ceiling of fronds covered the stage. The night was
hot and sultry as Isabel looped her arm through mine and we
passed the bubbling fountain of nymphets, water coursing
down their buttocks and thighs, cascading from their breasts
and hair.

Heads turned as we entered the large entryway. Isabel
looked straight ahead, clutching my arm. Her dress was sheer
white silk with a shawl that trailed behind her. I felt under-
dressed in my pink jumpsuit she'd asked me to wear, though
Isabel said when she saw me that I looked "stunning." That
was her word. Not one I'd usually apply to myself. Tonight,
instead of having her hair pulled back severely into a bun, as
usual, she wore it down, flowing to her shoulders. Everyone
turned to look at her.

Even emaciated, she could be a queen, the deposed ruler

of an ancient land. The crowds looked at her, because she was so regal. And because they knew who she was. She was the movie star, the celebrity in town, renowned not only for who her father was, but because she hated him so. She would tell it to anyone who asked, particularly foreign journalists. Suddenly lights flashed. Cameras went off. So now they had my face. Now everyone knew who I was as well.

"Your table is this way," the maître d' said. Isabel had made the reservations, arranged for the table near the stage, but off to the side so we wouldn't be disturbed. She had also arranged for the car to drive us from the hotel. My sense was that Isabel could arrange for anything, negotiate anything, except what she really wanted.

With a long drumroll the dancers rushed on. Swarthy men pranced with women dressed like aquatic birds. From our seats, I could see their painted-on eyebrows, smell their hair spray. Thighs, slightly flaccid, in mesh hose, were raised in my face. A long-legged woman in a peacock's tail strutted across the stage. Isabel poked the ice cube in her Cuba libre.

At nearby tables patrons whispered, nodding our way. Men in polished silk suits stopped at our table, offering Isabel their hands. A man who looked like Xavier Cugat appeared on stage. He had a thin mustache and a baton in his hand. Raising the baton, he struck up the band and shouted, "Now, everybody dance."

Grabbing me by the hands, Isabel pulled me to my feet. "Come on," she said. "Dance with me." She dragged me onto the dance floor, where she tipped her head back and began to sway. My face flushed as I felt the eyes of the room turn on us. Stroking me on the cheek, Isabel placed my hands on her waist. Then she drooped her hands around my neck.

Tossing her head back, she began to sway. I was surprised at how well she moved, how smoothly she led me across the floor. I tried to follow the steps, to move my feet in rhythm with hers. A few times I stumbled on her toes. Sweat appeared on her lower lip as she kept her gaze fixed on mine.

I wanted to look and see if other women were dancing together, but I couldn't take my eyes away from Isabel. She held me, guiding me across the room, and I could imagine her as she was—a little girl of no more than eight—the night her father came to dance with her.

It was close to two in the morning when we got back to the hotel and Isabel said she wanted to use the bathroom. She wanted to come upstairs. I was hot and sweaty and we were both a little drunk. She told the driver to wait for her and followed me up the stairs.

Inside the room, she flopped down on the bed. "Oh, it's so hot. I feel so dirty. Let's take a shower," she said. She pulled her dress over her head, stood there naked, then headed for the bathroom. I heard the water go on, the shower. Steam poured out of the bathroom. She called to me from inside. "Come," she said, "it will relax you."

As I passed the mirror, I couldn't see my face because of the steam. I rubbed my hand on it. I looked well, dark and tan. My hair had golden highlights, but under my eyes were circles. I never stayed up so late. Isabel's hand waved at me from behind the curtain. I slipped out of my dress and got in.

Water cascaded down her chest, her thighs. Her body was thin and yet round; there were soft curves, smooth lines. If she had more flesh, she would be beautiful, I thought. Here, she said, handing me the soap. I haven't bathed with a woman since Lydia and I washed together as girls. I had forgotten the smooth softness of the skin, the hairless flesh. Then she took the soap from me and had me turn around. Her long thin fingers ran up and down my spine. I loved the smooth circles her hands made on my shoulder blades, the even strokes down the backs of my legs.

Afterward we dried ourselves off. Isabel threw her hair forward, drying it briskly with the towel. Then she wrapped the towel around her waist and walked to the balcony, where she opened the French doors. We stood for a moment, drying off in the breeze. Then, exhausted and hot from the shower and from the heat of the night, we stretched out on the bed. She lay with her head resting against my shoulder and I let my fingers stroke her damp hair. My fingers moved between the strands, separating them. Her hair smelled fresh and I breathed it in until my breath quickened as I felt her skin against my skin.

Suddenly she sat up, pushing my hand away from her face. "What is it?" she said. "What do you want?"

"I don't know," I said, startled by her abruptness. "I don't want anything."

"You must want something," she said with an edge in her voice that left me feeling suddenly afraid. She was rising, staring at me from above. "You gringos are all alike. You are all selfish and afraid. You want adventures as long as there is no risk to yourself." She flung the covers back and was shouting now, grabbing for her clothes. "You think you are brave, but you are just like the rest of them. You are all stupid cowards."

She pulled on her dress and now she was sobbing, sputtering. I sat up, reaching for her across the bed, but she motioned me down. "Do you hear me?" she shouted, heading for the door. "You are all stupid, selfish cowards."

"You're wrong," I told her. "Isabel," I shouted, "don't leave." But she was heading, sandals in hand, for the door, which she slammed behind her. Wrapping a blanket around me, I went to the balcony and saw her car still waiting for her below. Her driver jumped out and opened the door for her. She slammed the door when she got in and the car sped off around the plaza, disappearing in the night.

Thirty

SOME MORNINGS I'll get up with the birds. In the oak tree out back dozens of birds roost and their morning calls wake me. In the spring there are the crows. But there are also the grackles, the starlings, the sparrows. When they wake me with their caws and cries and twitterings, I can't go back to sleep.

I'll look at Todd, asleep beside me in the chiaroscuro light. He sleeps on his back, mouth opening and closing. There are these odds moments of intimacy. When you can see the other, but he doesn't see you. Hair sticking every which way, the silly look of slumber on his face. Or a sudden flash of a dream passing behind his eyes. A glimpse of what he sees on the other side.

Then I'll pad downstairs, make myself a cup of coffee. This is my favorite time of day. Five-thirty or six A.M., no one up. I'll sip coffee, read the paper. There is a blue chair in the kitchen that looks out on the yard. I'll sit there, listening to the birds, wondering what would happen if Todd and Jessica woke up and found me gone. I'll wonder if I couldn't just pack a bag and leave. Where would I go? Of all the places to which I've traveled, which one draws me the most? That place in Maui accessible only by boat? The altiplano of Bolivia and Peru? Could I breathe that rarefied air for the rest of my life, groom alpacas, be accountable to no one?

When my coffee goes cold, I'll head upstairs. I'll pause at my daughter's room. The dog is asleep with his head on her pillow, and she clutches him in her arms. The dog looks at me and, knowing it isn't time to get up, puts his head back down again.

I'll go over, shove the dog aside. I'll slide between the covers on her bed, putting my body where the dog had been. I'll lie close to her and smell her milky breath, touch her soft skin. Unblemished. Perfect. I'll place my head down on the warm pillow and fall asleep.

A blaring telephone wakes me. I hear Todd's voice on the other end. "I think I should come down," he tells me. "This is taking too long."

Actually I have no idea how long it is taking. The days seem to melt into one. "I'm sure I'll be out of here in the next day or so."

"Maggie, it's been four days. Are you sure there isn't something you want to tell me?"

"What are you talking about? What do you mean?"

"It shouldn't take this long," he says. "Tell me. The last time you were there, what happened? What did you do?"

For two years now I have been silent. I have not told him a thing. He has no idea how close to the brink I came, how I teetered, then came back again.

"Nothing happened," I tell him, "nothing at all. But maybe you should come down." I am weeping into the phone.

"I'm going to," he says. "I'll be there. I'll come as soon as I can."

Thirty-one

FOR SEVERAL DAYS after our night at the Club Tropical I did not hear from Isabel. I did not try to find her after our fight and she did not try to reach me. I was making my way through the list of things I had to review. I had finished restaurants and museums. Hot spots and clubs were done. I had one or two joint-venture hotels on the north and south of the island to check out, but those were easy day-trips.

The historic walk through the old city was basically done and I had an afternoon walk to complete to the fortress by the sea, the site of the victory over the Spanish. If my work continued at its present pace, I would be done in three or four days. I considered going to look for Isabel but I had a great deal to attend to and found myself almost hoping that she would drift back into the shadows of my life as easily as she had appeared.

Just when I had resigned myself to this, I found her sitting in the lobby of my hotel one morning as I was heading out to do the walk to the fortress. I wasn't surprised to see her appear like this. She gave me a little nod when she saw me and I noticed that she looked pale, worse than she had when I first met her. Haggard, with deep circles beneath her eyes, as if she hadn't slept or eaten in days. I was surprised by the change that had overcome her. She was visibly altered, her eyes duller and dreamier than I had seen them, like someone who cannot recall who she is or what has happened to her. "You look terrible," I told her.

"I'm all right," she said, "no worse than usual." But she seemed despondent, downcast. "I have just got to get out of here. I have to get away." She grabbed me by the hands. "I really think," she said, "I think I will die if I have to stay."

"Come," I said, taking her by the hand over to the restaurant, where I ordered a glass of orange juice and a sandwich for her, though she assured me she couldn't eat. I sighed. "There must be something I can do for you."

"We scarcely know each other," she went on. "There is no point in you getting involved."

I reached across, stroked her hand. "I already am involved."

"Well, there *is* something. It is just that it is so much to ask . . ."

"You can ask," I said.

Her face shone. There was suddenly almost something beatific about her features. "You see, I have prayed for help," she began. "I have prayed for someone to come and deliver us and I have been beginning to think that no one would ever come. I have thought about this for such a long time now. It is almost all I do, but recently I have begun to think that perhaps it was you."

Now it is clear to me that when I saw her at the Church of

the Apparitions, she was praying for my help. Perhaps she had even told me to go there so that I would see her pray. I am not a religious person, but suddenly I felt that I had been sent, that it was my mission to deliver her. "What is it?" I said, leaning forward, our bodies almost touching.

She took a deep breath. "Well, this is what you could do, if you were willing. I'll just say it. Tell you what it is. You can listen and think about it. You could lose your passport and plane ticket. Three days later you will report them missing. During that time I will leave the country and your new passport and ticket will be issued. Manuel will make sure all this happens smoothly. If it costs you anything, I will repay you in the States."

I have blue eyes and coppery hair and I must weigh twenty pounds more than Isabel, but she says she has friends who will take care of these details. "You know who I am," she told me, "and you know who my father is, and there is no other way for me to go."

I have never lived particularly close to the edge. I like balanced meals, I put on my seat belt when I get into the car, even in the backseat. But suddenly I found myself tempted, not only because I wanted to help Isabel leave, but also because I wanted to stay. Not forever. It wasn't that I wanted to stay on *la isla* forever. Just for a little while—to dance until I forgot who I was and what I was doing there in the first place.

She would buy a sandy-colored wig and leave the country as me. And then who would I be? It was almost as if for a time—though I knew there was no logic in this—I would be Isabel. It makes no sense, but somehow I was being asked to trade places with her. This was something I knew how to do. It was a game I'd played before.

"What exactly would I have to do?" I asked as we sat in a café near the Miramar. Isabel wore her hair pulled back in a bun that made her bones stand out even more than they normally did. She sipped unsweetened lemonade and smoked a cigarette, which I had only seen her do when we first met.

"You would take a walk one night and sit by the seawall at a designated spot. Here you will leave your passport and ticket. Manuel will come by later and retrieve them. After that, we won't have any contact. You will wait until the day you are to leave and then report your documents missing. The Swiss embassy will provide you with new documents and you will leave as planned. They will consider it a theft. This kind of thing happens all the time here. It should go off without a hitch. I have friends who will make sure you leave and they will help me leave."

I had no idea why I was having this conversation with her. Why I was even toying with this idea. But there was something about Isabel—that look in her eyes, her hair pulled back like a refugee's. "If it was just me," I told her, "I'd help you, but I have my family to think of . . ." I thought of the tuition payment I had not made and all the responsibilities that I had assumed for myself. Everything suddenly seemed to weigh heavily on me.

Isabel was silent, staring at the table. "You'll be fine. I have people who will make sure . . ." I saw that familiar sadness settle over her features. A kind of fatigue, as if she had been through this so many times before. As if she knew she wouldn't be going anywhere.

Now she took out a cigarette and I stared at the pack. I hadn't even had the urge for one in years, but I reached across the table. She tipped the pack my way and I took one as

Isabel extended a match. Taking a drag, I was surprised at how good it tasted. How it seemed as if I'd never quit at all. It would be so easy to go back to this, I thought. Together we sat, smoking, without speaking. Soon my mouth tasted dry and a slight wave of nausea came. Slowly I put the cigarette out after a few drags. "I'm sorry," I told her, "but I don't think I can help you."

"No," she said, "of course you can't." The sadness like smoke wrapped itself around her again. "I didn't think you would."

Thirty-two

MANUEL lived down a few winding streets from my hotel, in the old city where laundry hung across the road. He led me along a narrow alleyway to a crumbling building that smelled of cooking oil and urine. The stairway had cats milling about, sucking on bones. His apartment was dark but Manuel pulled up the shade. He had a cot, two chairs around a card table, a sink, and a burner for cooking on the floor. The walls were decorated with fading posters, Miss Marimba 1984, Calle Ocho, the Esmeralda Band, Tito Puente.

Manuel opened the refrigerator, which contained a pitcher of fruit punch and a bottle of fifteen-year-old dark rum, and he began mixing tumblers with half of each, dropping in dirty ice cubes.

Despite the dinginess of the apartment, he had a decent record player and records and he was a natty dresser, with a closetful of silk suits and polo shirts, jeans and leather shoes. Never mind how he afforded them, he had what he needed.

He handed me a drink and motioned for me to sit beside him on the cot, which I was reluctant to do. I sat at the table and chair. "You gringas are all alike. You like to flirt. You tease, but you never really want anything." With a wave of his hand, he said, "Look at this dump. You have no idea what we have to do to live." He patted the place beside him on the cot, but I just stood in the center of the room.

"I don't think I can . . ." I said.

"What do you mean?"

"I don't think I can help her."

"You can do whatever you want," he said.

That night he took me to the Flamingo Club, for which he wore a lime green suit. We sipped planter's punch and danced every number. It was hot in the club, but under the strobe light I watched his feet move. They glided, changing as the music changed, and I did the best I could, following clumsily along.

A tango came on and he swept me up from the stool on which I sat. Bracing me with his hand, he led, taking long smooth strides, making sudden spins. Then he dipped me and I bent back farther than I thought I could bend.

"I know someone who can help you decide," Manuel said.

The Santero's house was hard to miss because it was freshly painted pink. On the lawn sat a huge carved statue of Santa Barbara and a satellite dish. Lesser saints with amulets, bouquets of dead roses lined the path. Manuel did not knock, but simply opened the door.

The service would not begin until midnight, when the gods change their sexes and Santa Barbara becomes Changó, the *santero*'s male god of war. Men and women dressed in flowing gowns, strewn with flower petals, sat before dishes of water, honey, egg yolk, and blood. They had sacrificed goats, chickens, and doves for the ceremony and the animals' remnants lay on the kitchen floor.

Angel, the *santero*, would take his seat soon. Space was made for me and Manuel. A woman in flowing purple began to chant and the *Babalao* appeared. He was dressed in red and his teeth shown gold. His skin was yellow and his hair a mass of greasy curls.

In the center of the room was a stool surrounded by candles. On the stool sat blood-filled plates, plastic dolls, carved wooden ships, statues of the Catholic saints, a crucifix, a bowl of passion fruit, mangoes, and tamarinds. Angel asked the gods if enough coffee, alcohol, and blood had been offered to satisfy them. He threw four square coconut chips on the floor. If two or more fell white-side up, then the answer was yes. The gods wanted brandy. A bottle was placed in the center of the room. Then Angel said he was ready.

"Nangaré, ñangaré, ñangaré," he chanted. Then the dishes with the swirling liquid were passed and I sipped from the water, the honey, the egg yolk. The blood swirled in front of me in the dish and I glanced at Manuel, who frowned, then gave me a nod of his head and I drank from that dish too, reeling as I felt the warm blood go down.

Angel dropped sixteen palm seeds into a powder-covered tray and studied the prints they made. For hours he tossed the palm seeds, studying the prints. The women swayed, chanting, and my head was spinning, as if I would faint. I tried to sit upright, but my legs ached and I longed to sleep.

The sun was coming up when Angel broke his silence and began to speak. Elegún, the god of destiny, says that you are to help Ochún, the goddess of rivers. This will enrage

Obatalá, the son of God, and he will bring Changó upon you, fire and war; Orisha cannot protect you from what you do.

What does this mean? I asked Manuel because I had no idea.

It means that you will help the girl, he told me, but there will be a price to pay.

Thirty-three

Y OU CAN'T underestimate the importance of shuttle buses. The traveler needs to feel that someone is waiting on the other end. Like children, we want a parent there when we race out of school. It is, of course, best when the hotel takes care of everything—the luggage, immigration, the transportation. But having the shuttle bus is what's most essential for me.

It is shuttle buses I am thinking of the morning Major Lorenzo does not show. I have grown accustomed to his punctual visits. The promise of him waiting for me on the other end of the night. The expectation that this day he will have my papers, my documents, an explanation in hand.

But this morning he does not arrive. I am surprised as I sit at my usual table. With every sound of footsteps, the door of the hotel opening, and the breeze blowing in, I look up and expect it to be he. Enrique is there that morning, but he does not wait on me. In fact, he appears to be ignoring me, because this is his usual table but he sends someone else over. I try to catch his eye, but he looks away and I think perhaps it is better if I do not bother him at all.

The usual crew is in the lobby. The Dutch boys are already drinking beer and cavorting with Flora and Eva. The dwarf sits, despondent, in a corner. Why do people want to go where they go? I wonder as I watch them all. I can understand taking the gourmet walking tour of Switzerland or the scenic cruise of the Nile. But why do they need to go to Vietnam after we tore the country to shreds, or to Romania? Do we really need to tell people that while the former Yugoslavia is no longer a possibility, Slovenia is? I grow despondent as I contemplate *Jungle Magazine*, sending their writer with a machete through the last stretch of virgin forest in the world. Kurt says his readers want to go everywhere, but I think to myself as I sit, waiting for Major Lorenzo, will they really want to come here?

The ceiling fans churn the sultry air as the tables begin to fill up. By eleven Major Lorenzo still has not appeared and all the tables are taken. Perhaps he is getting my papers in order. Perhaps he is just getting the necessary seals of approval, the required stamps, and then he will put me on the next plane. My plane will take off in a day or two and I'll be home that night. This misunderstanding will be cleared up at some embassy or another. Kurt will say it will make a funny article in a travel magazine. Or a sidebar in a "best/worst travel experience" column. Or he'll feel guilty and put me on the next plane to France.

The prostitutes spot me now and they wave. María arrived and for a moment the dwarf perked up, but she ignored him and he put his head down on the table, like a schoolboy at his desk. All three of them walk toward me together, María, Eva, Flora—I feel more and more certain these were the names of the birds on my dentist's drill. They pull over chairs and sit down. "So," María says, "we want to know everything. About New York. Miami. We want to get a VCR. I've got a sister up north. Once a year she sends me underwear, nail polish, and perfume. What's it like walking about with a Walkman on your head? Here people have got nothing to do so they fuck all day long. The problem is the natives can't pay us. No business there." She says this with a wide grin, revealing the space between her front teeth. Eva remains embittered about something and Flora keeps looking for customers. Since they have come to talk to me, business must be slow.

"You know," María goes on, "I didn't always do this. I used to be a secretary for a respected cabinet minister. And Eva, she worked for the airlines. Flora, well, Flora's got kids. I had this real good job, typing, pouring coffee during meetings. That sort of thing. Then my brother goes to the States on a hijacked plane and I have to take care of my mother and all the other kids. She had a bunch of them. So one day the minister tells me he knows all about my brother and I can keep my job if I wear short skirts to work. I don't know what to make of it, but I wear a short skirt the next day. Then he tells me if I want to keep working, I have to sit with my legs apart. I think who needs this. If I'm going to earn a living this way, I may as well really earn a living.

"There's really no point in being a prostitute here because what can you buy? On the black market, a few pairs of jeans, some gold jewelry. You see, what we really want—well, it's very simple—is someone who will get us out of here."

"Get you out of here?"

"Yeah, you know, marry us. Take us home with them."

"Do you really think . . ." I am astounded that they believe this could happen.

"We heard about a girl. She lived in Santiago and a German businessman took her back to Berlin. Foreigners love us. We are very exotic to them. And they tell us we treat them better than the girls back home."

"Well," I say with a smile, "if I could, I'd take you home with me."

We are laughing at this thought when Major Lorenzo walks in. The girls seem to sense him approaching and scatter like pods to the wind. He gives them a knowing smile, then nods my way. But I can see right away that something is wrong. There is no lilt to his step. His eyes are dull, as if he has eaten pig's fat or hasn't bicycled ten miles today.

"Well, Maggie, I am frustrated . . . ," he tells me as he sits down, "but there seems to be little progress with your case."

"What do you mean?"

"Well, I just can't get this paperwork through." Major Lorenzo seems embarrassed by this, sorry that he must disappoint me again. "And I'm afraid Jamaica is out of the question. The only place you can go is back to where you came from." As I contemplate the thought of being flown back to the frozen north, I notice once again that Major Lorenzo does not look me in the eye and I wonder if it is because he is ashamed or because he is lying. I almost would prefer it if Major Lorenzo were mean, not kind. At times it seems it would be easier with the colonel with the dead eyes, but he is long gone. Now, however, as I look at Major Lorenzo and realize that he too will not look at me, he reminds me of the colonel from the airport.

"Of course," the Major says, "it will straighten itself out.

We are looking into various solutions." But I am no longer listening to him.

"I think," I speak hesitantly, "that I really must contact my lawyer or an embassy official. I need to let someone know what's going on . . ."

Major Lorenzo frowns, looking hurt, as if I have doubted him. "Oh, that isn't necessary. Not at all. We'll have this matter cleared up in just a few days."

"But I still think . . ."

"Oh, you Americans." He throws up his hands. "You are in such a hurry to get things done." He rises to leave and smiles now, shifting his tone. "By the way," he says, "how is your daughter? Have you spoken to her?"

"She is fine," I tell him. "She wants me to come home."

"Yes, well, probably you will see her soon. They grow up so fast, don't they?"

"I wouldn't know," I tell him. "She's only five."

"Oh, you'll see, you blink and they're gone."

He looks wistful, as if he is remembering something far away, then says he'll be back in the morning, hopefully with my passport and plane ticket home. For the time being I remain like the people of *la isla*. With no passport; with no way out.

Later, when I go upstairs, I stand on the balcony of my room and I see the lines—people queued up for rations, for pizza, for ice cream, for the cinema. A throng waits for a bus and when it arrives they swarm like ants. For a while they hover, buzzing, while a few manage to shove their way on; then the bus drives away. The throng remains on the street, bewildered, and slowly I watch it disperse.

Thirty-four

ROSALBA sat chain-smoking in the lobby of my hotel, waiting in a yellow dress, prim and starched. When she saw me, she clasped my hands. "I don't have many options left to me now," Rosalba said. She had called to say she needed to meet with me. I had planned to finish my walk of the old harbor that day, which would complete my update for the city, but when Rosalba phoned she sounded so nervous and distracted that I agreed to meet her that afternoon. "I can't thank you enough," she said when she saw me. "I know how busy you are."

"Oh, it's nothing . . . You seemed to want to talk."

"Well, it means a great deal to me." Rosalba ordered another coffee and one for me. Then she lit another cigarette, her hands shaking as she smoked it. "I'm sorry. I'm not very well. I've been so worried about my daughter."

"The one in America?"

"Oh, no, she is fine, in a manner of speaking. No, Isabel.

You are a mother, you can imagine what it would be like. To watch your daughter destroy herself this way."

"Yes, I imagine it is."

Rosalba took a long drag. "Of course, you are a mother. You can understand. It is a terrible thing." Rosalba said there wasn't much time. "You must help me," she said. "I have only one daughter now. The other was taken from me long ago." And now Isabel, she said, was just wasting away.

Umberto Calderón's sister, Rosalba told me, lived in Biscayne Bay, and one December Umberto decided to take Serena there for Christmas. Rosalba packed her daughter's bag. She included the special things her oldest daughter loved—a polka-dot dress, a tattered teddy bear, a book of fairy tales she liked to read, a deck of cards with animals on the back. In a small zippered compartment of Serena's suitcase, Rosalba slipped in an envelope that contained a photograph of herself, one of Isabel, and another of Mercedes. She scrawled a note: "So you'll have something to remember us by." Rosalba tucked the envelope into the compartment, zipping it shut.

It would not be until years later, as Serena was getting ready to go off to college, that she would find this envelope with the photographs and her mother's note hidden in a side pouch of one of her suitcases. This would only confirm Serena's belief that her mother had known all along. She knew that her daughter would not return, but instead would clasp to her the objects her mother had so carefully packed and would weep into the night. She'd weep until she could weep no more and then she would grow into a woman who would spend her life in department stores, shopping for things she did not need. Or that Umberto Calderón would never practice dermatological medicine again, but instead would sell small parcels of the Florida coast.

This would leave him a wealthy but broken man who had expected that at any moment during the last years of his life he would return to the house by the sea. Even after he learned that Rosalba had long ago given the house over to the Department of Public Works, he dreamed that he would go home, and he died with the keys in his pocket.

Serena carried the envelope with the pictures everywhere she went—and in it she held on to her rage. This envelope assured her that as her mother packed her bags she knew her daughter would grow up to speak a language that was not her own and go to Disney World and cruise Calle Ocho. That they would meet years later when Serena began to make her annual visits and find themselves face-to-face with little to say to each other, except that Serena would take out the envelope and photographs and hold it in her mother's face and say, "You knew, Mother, didn't you? You knew we were never coming back."

"No, I really didn't." Which Rosalba swore was true.

"You are a liar," Serena said.

After Serena was gone, Rosalba knew that El Caballo had come to see Isabel. She had not noticed it before, but now she knew because there was only the two of them in the big house by the sea, except for Mercedes, who was old now and slept most of the day. Isabel would dance, twirling dreamily through the empty rooms of the big house, and Rosalba was certain he had come to try and take this child away as well.

Rosalba had put up with his insomnia, his useless cures of valerian root and mullein, his late-night pontificating to the maids, his erratic comings and goings. She had even put up with all his other women. But what she could not put up with was the thought that he would try and take her child away. She would have nothing left.

She went to the small apartment where she had once waited for him in the waning light of the day when the sun would burn orange through the window. She put on the radio and listened to his voice as she packed the silken sheets they had once slept on, the coffee cups they had sipped from. She put into boxes the magazines she had read while waiting for him and the negligees she had greeted him in. And then she packed the radio and dragged the boxes, one at a time, down to her car.

She left the door open with a note on it that this apartment had been abandoned and that she hoped a family would settle in. Months later she would stop by the old apartment that had been her love nest. Two dark children would answer, snot running from the noses, the smell of cooking oils coming from inside.

She packed up the big house as well, having relinquished it to the Department of Public Works, which would turn it into administrative offices. She took only what she needed, leaving the rest behind. The upholstered sofas and damask curtains. She took the porcelain from Spain and the silver that had been in Umberto Calderón's family for centuries in case he ever came back and asked for his mother's silver. She took the paintings that framed the entryway and two suitcases of clothes for herself. Two more for Isabel.

The personal effects that belonged to Serena and Umberto Calderón she left behind, putting them into boxes in the basement of the great house. If they ever returned, they would find the boxes there, though once she returned and found they had been mostly picked through and carted away.

She only took keepsakes—a brooch she had received as a wedding gift, Serena's christening gown.

Then she put Isabel in the car, kissed good-bye a weeping Mercedes, who would return to relatives in the eastern provinces she had not seen in years. Isabel sobbed and pleaded, throwing herself at her mother's feet, but there would be no room for Mercedes. They were going back to live with Rosalba's mother in the same house where Rosalba grew up in the Miramar—the house that the revolutionary housing authorities had divided into four small apartments. For many years, until Isabel had a family of her own, the three women lived in the apartment that had once been their living and dining rooms.

Rosalba knew that if she went to El Caballo, if she begged him, he would let her leave. But she could not do this because when she was a girl, her mother had taken her out to the sugarcane plantations in the east and she had seen a boy with coiled limbs crawl toward her and beg. He lived in a row of cardboard boxes and tin-roofed shacks. On one of the tin roofs a woman lifted her skirts and spread her legs, begging to be paid.

There are no beggars, now, Rosalba would tell anyone who asked. Look around you. We all have houses. Everyone has food. No one is really starving, except my daughter, Rosalba said.

Thirty-five

I DON'T KNOW how long Manuel has been watching, but he is amused to find me with María, Eva, and Flora. "Thinking of changing professions?" he asks. "Certainly it must be more lucrative than doing updates for travel guides." He had watched them scatter when Major Lorenzo arrived.

"Listen," I tell him, "I'm not sure what's going on, but Lorenzo says there are delays."

"Scare tactics, I told you," Manuel says. "They just want to frighten you. Believe me, you'll be on that flight Saturday morning."

"I'm not so sure . . ."

"Maybe you need to relax," he says, touching my brow, "take it easy for a while. Are you getting enough rest?"

"I'm getting plenty of rest," I say, brushing his hand away.

When I get upstairs, I pick up the phone to call Jessica and tell her I'll be home soon. I am surprised when she answers. I decide I'll really confuse whoever is listening, carry on this conversation in code. "It's Mommy," I tell her, "who's home with you there?" Of course I know that Todd is. We split everything down the middle. When I am away, he brings her home. "What are you doing there, Mommy? Have you been to the zoo? Do they have tigers?"

"No," I tell her, "no tigers, just vultures." I am not making this up; I've seen them.

Now Todd gets on the phone. "Are you all right?" he asks. "Can you talk?"

"I'm not sure," I answer. "Probably not."

"Look, Maggie, I checked into flights, but there's nothing coming down until next week."

"Oh, it's all right," I tell him. "I'll be home by then."

"Well, I'm going to call Kurt; I think it's time—"

"Honey, he can't do anything. In a day or two I'll be home; there's no need to worry."

Sometimes at night I'll stand in front of the mirror, examining my body for flaws. Battle scars. "Don't you see what's wrong with me?" I'll ask him.

"I only see what's there." When he realizes this answer doesn't satisfy me, he'll say, "I love you the way you are."

"Which way is that?" I'll ask.

Thirty-six

THE CEILING FANS turned overhead, and it promised to be another warm, muggy day. I had ordered the breakfast buffet—dry toast, white asparagus, runny eggs, a slab of bacon, pineapple out of a can. Nescafé. Pineapple out of a can? Nescafé? I asked Enrique as he put it down. He shrugged a what-can-I-do shrug.

With my itinerary for the day set before me, I was just settling down to eat when Isabel came in. There was an optional walking tour of colonial architecture I planned to do and an exhibit of postrevolutionary paintings in the lobby of the Hotel Nacional. Then I was going to rent a car and check out a few beaches to the west. A small rain forest that had been given a "worth the detour" in our last edition.

Isabel did not see me, but I saw her as she rushed into the lobby, the eyes of the staff following her. There was an urgency to her movements, a need to be somewhere. She wore a pink pajamalike outfit and her dark hair was down. Dark green sunglasses. I heard the click of her sandals on the mosaic tiles. Whom did she remind me of at this moment? Mata Hari? Isadora Duncan?

She went to the desk, where she leaned forward to ask the young clerk something, and I saw him pointing my way. In another hotel in another country, I would think this was an example of good service. Instead it made me uncomfortable that they knew where I was.

Enrique was coming by to top off my coffee as Isabel waved and smiled. His face grew sullen and he stepped away. Now she stood breathless in front of my table. "Are you ready?" she asked.

"For what?"

"Don't you remember? There is a fiesta for my twin cousins. They are sixteen today."

I am fairly good at remembering invitations. I write them down. I don't forget dates, events, doctors' appointments. I stared at my eggs, which were runny, swirling in the plate. I thought about the walking tour of colonial architectural sights I was to take that afternoon. The seafood restaurant along the shore where I was to sample—and risk hepatitis or worse—local shrimp. "Just let me get a few things," I said.

Enrique looked at me sadly, as if by not finishing my breakfast I had offended him. I was wasting food; this was not a country in which to waste food. I wolfed down the egg, canned pineapple, white asparagus while Isabel went to make a phone call. While she was gone, Enrique asked me, "You know what you're doing, don't you?"

"Of course I do," I said.

"Be careful," he said. This time he did not whisper.

I changed into a thin cotton dress, put my camera into a bag. Isabel was waiting for me in the lobby when I came down. She was ebullient, glowing. She wrapped her arm around me and we left, the eyes of the hotel staff on my back.

This time we took the northern road out of town, one I'd never been on before. "First we have some stops to make," Isabel said, driving off the main road. Here the houses were more like shacks, bits of tin and cardboard banged together with slabs of wood, dirt floors. Barefoot children in tattered clothes waved at us from the side of the road as we pulled up in front of a large building, lined with bars. Were the twin cousins in jail? For a moment I was frightened, but the sign above the gate said it was the Zoológico Antiguo.

I got out and peered through the fence into cages that appeared empty, except for a lonely tapir that stood motionless, its snout pressed to the bars, and a pair of vultures that sat on a log, though I wasn't sure if they were part of the display. "I'll just be a minute," Isabel said, clutching a small cardboard box.

I didn't really want to roam through a zoo of empty cages and despondent animals. "I'll wait for you here." While I waited, the tapir watched me, sniffing the air, as if it had not seen a visitor in a long time.

Then Isabel returned, sweat on her brow, and handed me a box that was full of sticky candy. We got back into the car and she drove farther, until she came to a funeral parlor and once again she jumped out, leaving me holding the box, and said she'd be right back.

This time she returned with colored paper, the kind florists use for wrapping flowers. "Here," she said, "we need to wrap the candy. It's the least we can do."

Though I wasn't sure how Isabel was related to the twins, as she drove, I wrapped the candy. I tore off strips of the colored paper and picked up each sugary ball, folding the red

or green or yellow plastic paper around it, packing each carefully back in the box. My hands grew moist and sticky as we
drove for perhaps an hour, until we came to a small village.

We turned up a dusty road to a circle of cinder-block
buildings. The Juventud de la Revolución development park,
it was called. "There are things you should see," Isabel said.
"They won't be on your walking tour. They won't be on any
tour of this country. But perhaps you will find room for this
in your guidebook. Perhaps you can slip this into the chapter
on joint-venture hotels."

She parked on the side of a dirt road and we walked
through the rows of houses. I peered inside the one-room
shacks where all the televisions were on. People sat, bleary-
eyed in the middle of the day, drinking beer in front of the
TVs. A soccer match was on, but from time to time the voice
of El Líder spoke, urging the people to work hard for the
revolution, to pick their sugarcane crop, to mine for nickel,
to practice birth control, to send the children to school, to
serve in the armed forces and fight for the state.

"You hardly ever see his face," Isabel said. "Have you
noticed? There are no pictures of him; no posters. But you
hear him. He's like your Wizard of Oz. I only have to turn
on the television, I can hear my father. He is everywhere, like
God. That is his great gift. He is everywhere and nowhere."

The fiesta for the Jiménez twins, Alivira and Eduardo, for
their sixteenth birthday, was taking place in the town square,
where music screeched over speakers set up on rooftops. Old
men drank beer on the steps of the houses that lined the
square. On a rickety picnic table sat a pink cake, decomposing in the sun. A few children sat around the picnic table, but
no one played. Their eyes lit up when we put the box of

candies, procured from the zoo and the funeral parlor, in front of them.

It had taken three weeks to get the cake, Isabel told me, because you must go to the special office for birthday cakes; and then there is a special ration store for sodas. The balloons were a gift from the Chinese, who had sent a million condoms, too small for the men of *la isla,* but perfect for use as birthday balloons.

I walked past a broken-down carousel—its ancient horses toppling over—and rows of inflated condoms, painted with poster paint. Over the loudspeaker salsa music blared. A Beny Moré tape played in another house. The Jiménenz twins danced together to a slow waltz like lovers in the corner. Their mother, a very large woman, danced with an older son. Their father had been in jail for fifteen years; they saw him at Christmas and on his birthday.

"You see how we live," Isabel says. "This is not what you'll find at your joint-venture hotels. This is not what they'll let you see anywhere. You want to see a cigar factory; they'll take you to a model cigar factory. You want to see a hospital emergency room; they'll take you to a model emergency room. But if you want to see how we really live, then you must come here."

Men and women milled about. No one seemed to know what to do. I was a curiosity, so several came up to me. One young blind boy touched my face. "American?" an old woman asked in disbelief. I was handed a plate of potato stew with some chicken bits floating in the sauce. I wasn't hungry, but I ate it anyway.

"Come on," Isabel said. "I want to take you somewhere." There was a hill that rose behind the town square and on the top of that hill was an old fortress, overlooking the sea. "I want you to see the view."

We climbed slowly through the ragweed and thick grass until we reached the ruins of the old fortress. "You see, it was from here that the country was defended during the Spanish-American War. You know, the war when the Americans came to help us, but then somebody made a mistake and they flew your flag. That was the beginning of the end for my country."

Then she took me by the hand and led me through a passageway that smelled of urine and rum. We went down several broken steps where creatures scurried away. When we came out, we stood on the rise of a cliff jutted out over the sea. "It was near here," she went on, "that my second husband drowned. He was a *balsero* and I watched him build his raft. I told him he was crazy and he told me he'd send for me from Florida. Pieces of his raft drifted ashore just a few hours after he sailed and I came here with a *santero*, who floated candles on the sea. The *santero* followed the candles until they stopped a few miles up the shore. That was where his body washed up the next day."

The fortress had a musty smell; its walls were covered with moss. Isabel led me up a small crumbling staircase until we reached a parapet with a view of the sea. We stood there, the wind blowing in our faces, the sun burning our skin. "Whenever I come here," Isabel said, "I think I know what it is to feel free."

We stood on the top of the cliff and Isabel set her eyes to the north. She looked beautiful, in her pink pajamas, the breeze blowing through her hair. The sea breeze filled my lungs.

Once when we were girls, Lydia and I took our walk

through the woods and went farther than we had ever gone. Lydia kept wanting to turn back, but I urged her to keep going. We followed the stream behind our house until we came to a bluff high above a lake that we didn't even know was there. We stood amazed at the vast expanse of water before us and I suddenly knew that there was a world larger than any I had envisioned and it was not that far from where we lived. I thought that I could just take Lydia and we could go off across that lake and if we wanted we could get to the other side. But then Lydia squeezed my hand as she always did when she was ready to turn around, so after a little while we made our way home.

"I want to help you," I told Isabel as we stood at that cliff overlooking the sea. "You must tell me what to do." She put her arm around my shoulder and pulled me to her. She kissed me firmly on the lips. I could taste her lipstick, which had a strawberry flavor, and smell her perfume, which was too strong and perhaps stale.

Thirty-seven

AT NIGHT there are noises in the room next door. A party is going on. I hear drinking, laughter, voices rising. I try to sleep, but it is useless. I put the pillow over my head. Finally I can't stand the noise. I decide to go knock on the door and ask them to please be quiet. I go into the hall, but there is no one there. I put my ears to the doors of rooms, but no sound comes. Manuel is right, I tell myself. I am losing my mind. I am suffering from captive's syndrome. Everything that is happening I am making up.

I ask the operator to make a collect call to the States. It is the middle of the night, but Todd answers the phone. Maggie, he says, what is it? Are you all right?

This will really get them, I think, if they are listening in. I'm fine. I'm sure I'll have my papers in the next day or so. I'll be home by the weekend. This is just a misunderstanding. It will be cleared up soon. Listen, I tell him, do you remember when we were living in separate cities? You were in Boston that winter. Do you remember what we did? There is a palpable pause on the other end. I hear Todd clearing his throat.

"I want you to make love to me on the phone. I want you to tell me what you'd do to me if I were there." Of course, if I were there, we'd probably be sound asleep, like children nestled in each other's arms, because we are so tired from our lives that making love has become a luxury. But now my hand moves over my breasts, between my legs. "Where would you put your hands? What would you do with your tongue?"

"I can't do this now . . . ," Todd says, but his voice is breathless, faint.

"Then I'll do it. I want you to suck on my breasts, I want to feel your tongue between my legs . . ." I try, but it isn't working. It isn't working not because I know someone is recording this call, but because Todd doesn't seem to want to. I don't really think that Todd is seeing Sarah, that woman from his office, but at this moment, just at this moment, I think that he is. Though this could never happen to me, I imagine that my husband isn't alone. That someone else is there.

Suddenly I picture Lyle Nashe's suitcase open and in his miniature crime scene I see my dishes, my furniture, my dog. But who is the masked man, peering into the window? Who is that masked man, coming up the stairs?

Thirty-eight

"NOW, MRS. CONOVER, let's go back to the beginning," the fat man says as he sits on the edge of his desk, his legs spread. I cannot bring myself to look at him or to look up at his thick legs, down into his round, bulging crotch. I am afraid that the wrong move, an unsure gesture, an indiscreet glance will be misconstrued. I am back in the same gray cinder-block room where Major Lorenzo first brought me. The same barbed-wire-surrounded building. Once again Major Lorenzo waits for me outside.

Except for a secretary, taking notes, I am alone in the room with this man. "Can you describe for me the circumstances under which you met Isabel Calderón?"

"I met her at the airport and a friend introduced us."

"But she left with a passport and a ticket and you reported yours missing . . ."

"I believe it was stolen from me. Or somehow I lost it."

The fat man sighs, rubbing his face. Sweat covers his brow

and when he takes his hands away, his skin glistens. Behind me there is a rustling of papers. The room is stifling with a smell of bodies that makes me think of tawdry encounters, unmade beds. "Why don't you tell us," he says, "what you are doing here. And then you can go home."

"I'm working for a travel-guide company, Easy Rider Guides. I go to countries and revise the guidebooks." I repeat the phrases as if I have memorized them by rote. And what is Easy Rider Guides? A cover for what or whom? "Beaches, hotels, restaurants," I tell him. That is my beat.

"And the first time you came here . . ." He leans forward, resting his hands on the file in front of him. "What was the purpose of your visit that time?"

He has asked me the same questions dozens of times and we go around in the same circles. Even now as I talk to him, I am vague about what really happened. Did my papers just tumble through the rocks and off into the sea? Or did someone retrieve them as we had planned? I'm sure whatever I did was purposeful, yet it feels like an accident as I sit here now. This confusion brings me to tears and once I start crying I find I cannot stop. Like a flood that has opened, I weep and weep. "I'm sorry," I manage to say. "It's just that I feel as if I've been away so long. I miss my daughter."

"We understand," the man says. "This is a country where many people miss their daughters. You'll be able to go home soon. Now, shall we go back to the beginning?" he says. "I assure you we have plenty of time." He takes out a cigarette and offers me one. I am tempted, but somehow I know this is not the moment to give in. I quit, I tell myself. I have quit many things. "You have been here before, have you not, Mrs. Conover?"

"Yes, I have . . ."

"And what was the purpose of your visit that time?"

"I've already told you . . ."

"But you made contact with Isabel Calderón, did you not?"

"I met her on a few occasions."

"And would you say you were instrumental in helping her leave?"

"I don't even know," I tell him quite truthfully now, "that she is gone."

He gives me an exasperated look that I have seen in the faces of officials before. Border guards and policemen get this look. My allotted time is up and now he will decide what is to be done. He has lost interest in me, the way a dog does with a toy it has been tossing around.

"Mrs. Conover, it is our strong belief that you provided your passport and plane ticket to Isabel Calderón, thus enabling her to leave this country. That you did this knowingly and willingly and are therefore guilty of something, perhaps it is not a crime, but it is a deception. But that you helped her, of that we feel certain."

I too have grown bored with these proceedings, but suddenly I feel as if I am fighting for my life and I have to garner every ounce of my strength to fight this battle. "Sir, if I am guilty of anything, it is carelessness. But where I come from this is not a crime." I manage to say this without really telling a lie. I have been careless in many ways; this time it is easy to tell the truth.

He takes a sip from a glass on his desk and my mouth feels parched. "You realize that there is a flight out in a day's time. I'm sure you'd like to be on that flight."

"I would very much like to be on that flight."

"Well," he says, holding out his hands.

"I've told you everything I know." Tears I cannot seem to control stream down my cheeks and he looks almost as if he believes me.

Thirty-nine

THERE WAS a moment when I would have done anything for you. When I couldn't do enough. I would have lied, cheated, betrayed. When you called me a coward, I knew I would have taken any risk. When you said I was weak, I knew I would be strong. I could tell a lie. I could keep a secret. I could tell your story. I easily could have allowed your drama to become my life. Perhaps I even would have allowed you to become my life.

What drew me to you wasn't your body or your breasts, not your laughter or your rage. It was the story you had to tell. I was certain I would see you again. That you would come and find me wherever you were. Now I can only imagine what happened next. I can only imagine what became of you after I was gone.

Forty

PERHAPS Isabel examined her body, naked before the mirror. She saw bones wrapped in skin, a prisoner of war who had refused all food. The veins in her legs were like those in an egg yolk when the chick has started to form. Her arms dangled like a classroom skeleton's. Suddenly she saw herself the way her mother, her daughter, the men who still slept with her from time to time saw her. She knew this was not good. She had to prepare, to train for what lay ahead.

She ate ice cream, rich in butterfat, and pizza, which was easily had. At first she vomited the grease that slid down her throat, the richness in her belly. But then she moved on to pork chops when she could find them, *papas* and plantains, all fried. This was once a country of appetites and now hers suddenly returned. She found she was hungry again and wanted to devour everything in sight. But she was hungry for what she could not have. *Caramelo, carne asada, arroz con pollo.* The tastes of her childhood. She wanted paella, brimming with sweet sausage and lobster. *Fettucini o muerte* was the revolutionary slogan she wrote across her wall. She contemplated a menu of sirloin, wild rice, creamed spinach. Uttering the words *charlotte russe*, a dish she had never had before, made her mouth water.

Isabel had lived on cheese and grass for years—grazing food. Lettuces, dandelion greens. Now she reveled in the fat of meat, the heaviness of potatoes. She ate tubers and felt hefty, closer to the ground. She was in training. The gringa had allowed herself to be kissed on the lips and Isabel knew that this time she would not be let down.

In the evening she waited for Milagro to return from her father's. Isabel had an affection for Ernesto. He had been, and still was, a very good man. And she believed he had loved her. They all had loved her—except, of course, El Caballo. And so she could not love any of them back.

Isabel waited in the yard for Milagro to come home. She stood under the trees where she had slept with her daughter in her arms. She could smell the jasmine, the acacia sap. The brilliant purple blooms of the *framboyán* almost dared her to leave. This was not the garden where she had once picked passion fruit and papaya from the tree, but she could still pick tamarind and *acerola*. She caressed the exploding red flower of the weeping bottlebrush, touched the maze of the screw pine. The fishtail palm really looked like fish tails. How can I leave this place, she wondered. She had never felt wool against her thin skin. She had hardly lived anywhere except in her mother's house.

She was going to leave all this behind. Her mother, her daughter, even her father. She was going to get on a plane and fly away and never look back. It would be the easiest thing in the world to do.

Milagro's footsteps approached, her feet on the stone path,

through the leaves of the *júcaro* tree. The sky over the city was indigo and pale orange. Milagro was always on time and Isabel took her by the hand. It was dusk in Ciudad del Caballo. Cars sputtered home from work. Together they made their way through the streets, down alleyways. They walked until they came to a crumbling house near the sea.

It was the house where Isabel once slept in a room of yellow curtains with a cat named Topaz, where her father came to dance with her. Now it was an administration building for the Department of Public Works. But Isabel knew the way up the back stairs to the roof. She had been coming here all the time when the offices were closed, which was most of the time.

On the roof with its vista of the sea Isabel and Milagro began their routine. They stretched their arms high over their heads. Breathing deeply, they stretched higher, then dropped down, touching their toes. They spread their feet and reached again for their toes in long even strokes, like two pendulums in synchronicity.

Then they lay on the floor, feet touching, holding hands. Isabel sat back and Milagro pulled her up; then Milagro sat back and her mother tugged her up. They did this fifty, one hundred, two hundred times. They began again, only this time they did not hold hands. Two hundred sit-ups, two hundred push-ups. They panted and sweat.

Isabel picked up a heavy wire cable and handed Milagro a tire iron. They slapped themselves across the backs and legs. The whacks were sharp, like someone being flogged, but the women did not cry out. "This is nothing," Isabel said to her daughter. "We must be brave, *mi hijita*. We must prepare ourselves for what lies ahead."

Forty-one

LATELY Mummy's been acting strange. Not that she's not always strange, but now she does things she's never done before. Like when I play Calle Ocho really loud she tells me to turn it down. No more pirated music. Even Tito Rodgríquez and my punk-salsa bands—*los metálicos*—she wants me to turn down. She wants everything quiet. No disturbances, she says. At night she closes the house up tight so nobody can see in. She's playing it—how do you say?—close to the vest.

Mummy has always been very obvious about everything. She wears bright colors—hot pink and orange. And she doesn't care who hears her or what they say. Her laugh is so loud you think something is wrong. Then last week not only does she want everything quiet, but she starts eating too. Before, a carrot stick and lemonade, that was lunch for Mummy. Now she cooks things that made her throw up before. Sticky pastries. Fat-rich stews. Pork rind, potatoes, dough bread. Smells that never came from our kitchen are coming from there now and suddenly I come home to silence and pots cooking on the stove.

Once I read this story about a girl whose father was becoming a plant. His blood was green. Leaves grew from his head. That's how I feel about Mummy. Not that she's becoming a plant, but she's not the same form of life she was a few weeks ago. Now she could almost sprout teeth and hair and start prowling at night.

I go about my business. Pretend nothing is wrong. With Chico like always I go to the sea. We sit on the seawall, smoke a joint. He cops a feel. Then we beg pencils and stuff off the tourists. Sometimes we score big. A pair of jeans, a heavy-metal T-shirt, and nobody expects much in return. It's amazing what people will give you if you ask just right. Once a lady gave me a sweatshirt that read "Try Our Buffalo Wings," but nobody knows what it means. I've gotten candy bars, cans of tuna, shampoo. Of course, technically, we don't need anything at all. If Mummy would just get on her knees and grovel, we could have whatever we wanted. Be the dutiful daughter, keep your big mouth shut. But Mummy has always said whatever she wanted, whatever popped into her little head.

Like just last year when the surveillance men were across the street from our house all the time. They pretended they were doing road repairs, but why, tell me, when all the main streets of *la isla* have potholes big enough you could land a spaceship in them, would they bother to repair the potholes on our little deserted side street? So Mummy goes up to them each day and tells them that their *líder* is an *estúpida* and why don't they do something useful like blow up his house. They just stare at her and sometimes they grin, then go about their business, fixing the road.

But now suddenly it's all different and Mummy is silent as if there's some big secret around here and you open your mouth and it will jump out of her head. But I am no *estúpida*. I can see things as they are. I know by the way she sips these stews and fills the house with the petals of roses and cowrie shells, the way she lights candles to Madre de Caridad, that something is going to happen. You don't have to be a genius to see that Mummy is tossing out old clothes, throwing away what she doesn't need anymore. Since she's a bit of a pack rat, when she starts to throw things out, that's when I know. She thinks she's going somewhere, but for once she's not talking about it and I know better than to ask.

Anyway, I don't need to. Because that's the one thing about me and Mummy. She can't fool me.

Forty-two

I T IS LATE in the day when Major Lorenzo brings me back to my hotel. The afternoon light is waning, the birds are returning to roost in the trees above the plaza. He asks if there is anything I need and I beg him to take me around, show me the sights. A quick visit to the fortress. "Please," I beg him, "just let me take a short walk by the sea."

He shakes his head because that is what he cannot do. "I wish I could. I understand how you are feeling." I wonder how he could understand, but then he asks with concern in his voice if I will be all right.

"Yes, I suppose I will." My eyes are burning, my skin stings from the salt of my tears.

When Major Lorenzo drops me off, I invite him in, but he refuses. He says it gently, but somehow I feel as if something has changed between us. "Wouldn't you like a coffee?" I say. He points to his Rolex watch and says he must be getting home. I try to picture Mrs. Lorenzo—a short, stout woman, built close to the ground, preparing a mutton stew with rice and beans. Or perhaps I would be surprised. Perhaps she is tall and European. He lusts after her all the time.

"That's a nice watch," I tell him.

"Yes," he says, "it was a gift from a colleague." He doesn't say which colleague.

"You don't have trouble getting nice watches like that here?"

"No, there is very little we have trouble getting." He opens the car door for me. "You'll be all right," he says, "won't you?"

"Yes, of course I will."

The prostitutes are sitting at a table in the bar and they wave at me as I walk into the lobby. I find I am actually glad to see them, happy to see familiar faces. It seems as if the prostitutes have accepted me as one of their own. They don't exactly understand it, but since I seem to more or less always be in the hotel like them, they decide I am an international operator. They motion for me to join them for a beer, which of course I will buy.

"Hey," Flora says, "why don't you come out with us tonight? We can drum up some business for you."

"We see you went out with the commandant today," Flora says with a smirk on her face. "Did you have a good time?"

They are joking, but then they seem to notice that my eyes are red, that something is wrong. "Hey," María says, offering me a seat. There is something about her that I like, the gentleness of her features. She is so small and petite, always in the same red dress, her friendly smile, like someone I'd be happy to have baby-sitting for Jessica, telling her when bedtime is, what stories to read. "You've been crying," she says.

"Actually I'm not in a very good situation."

She pulls a chair back and I sit down beside her. Her face is filled with concern. "What is it?" she says, "What did you do?"

I don't know why it is, but I need to confide. "The last time I was here," I tell her, "I helped someone leave."

She gasps, catching her breath. "Ah," she sighs, "I see."

"Now I don't know what will happen. I don't know when they'll let me leave."

"Who was it?" she asks. "Who did you help go?"

I almost tell her, but then I think better of it. "It was nobody," I tell her, "nobody you'd know." She nods, a look of disappointment on her face that seems more extreme than the situation warrants.

Later I return to my room. As I approach the door, I see a small object leaning against the jamb. It is a little doll made of cloth, dark, with black hair. A scrawny, unappealing doll, though it looks vaguely familiar to me. I cannot imagine who left it here, or why. I'm not sure if its purpose is to protect me or harm me, but I take it inside. I put it on my dresser, turning it this way and that. Then it occurs to me that from a certain angle as I look at its dark hair, its stick-figure form, this doll could be Isabel.

Forty-three

THOUGH they rarely ate together, this night they would. Rosalba had a pot cooking on the stove. Chicken, rice, and peas. Isabel arrived with a bowl of flower petals and incense, talismans around her neck. Milagro wore a Disneyland T-shirt and carried with her a small stuffed bear. A faint odor of tobacco and a feeling that someone had recently been there filled the room. Isabel sniffed like a dog. "Who was it, Mother?" And then she asked again, more insistently. "Did he come and see you again?"

"No, *mi hija*, he did not come," Rosalba said, "but I will tell you this. Your father is going to die."

"We are all going to die," Isabel said.

"But he is going to die soon."

"So let him die and take his whole goddamn country to hell with him."

Rosalba shuddered. She knew that when she approached her daughter, Isabel turned cold, as if Rosalba had done something Isabel could not forgive. She had seen Isabel's laughter turn dull when Rosalba entered a room and seen her daughter recoil at her touch. It was what Umberto Calderón taught her, Rosalba assumed. He taught all these ways of pushing away. We learn the most from those who do not want us, Rosalba knew.

"He was a man of great dreams," Rosalba said. "You have no right to say these things."

"I hate this place," Isabel said. "I hate him. And I hate what I have become."

Then Rosalba raised her gnarled hands, her joints like the burls of old trees, the only part of her that betrayed her age. "There is no use fighting over this," she said. Then she turned to Isabel. "If you can," she said, "you will go."

That night as Rosalba sat on her patio, feeling the sultry breeze, she knew that soon her second child would leave her and probably her granddaughter too and she would be left alone. She thought how Isabel would take the eyes of El Caballo with her when she went. Once El Caballo said to her, Rosa come with me and we will change the world, but she was a woman with two children to raise. How could she go? A man cannot understand this.

She was with him for more than a dozen years and had thought about him every day since she was sixteen years old. That is a lifetime. Before she left the apartment that had been their love nest, she went to the *botánica*, where she bought votive candles, which she lit in every corner of their rooms. She bought new floor washes—Go Away Evil and Never Look Back. Rosalba scrubbed the floor and the walls as high as she could reach. She washed every inch of that apartment, then bathed in Love Leave Me bath oils.

She cut pieces of her hair and the traces she found of his. She found bits of a fingernail, flower petals, dust motes under the bed. All this she burned in a small bowl. But Rosalba knew even as she sat on her patio, breathing in the breeze through the tamarind and jasmine trees, that there was this part that she could never wash or burn. And even if Isabel went and took what little she had left of him, or of anything in this world, this part would remain.

Forty-four

THE NIGHT I was supposed to leave my passport and ticket by the seawall, the streets were deserted in Puerto Angélico, though it wasn't late, just after nine. I walked slowly, as if I were only out for an evening stroll, and listened to my own footsteps clicking on the cobblestone. I rarely walk alone at night in New York and so the sound of my footsteps surprised me. Only lovers and a few solitary souls were out that night, but no one paid any attention to me and I knew what it felt like at last to be invisible.

It was a balmy night and the moon was high and I wished Isabel were with me. The last time I saw her, she had told me that we would not meet again on *la isla*. That she would see me, as she put it, on the other side.

I walked a hundred paces past the fortress until I found the place where the two broken slabs of concrete made a cradle. Here I sat on the seawall and gazed out to sea, letting my bag rest on the wall and slip between the boulders that held back the water. After a few moments I dug down and found the tickets and my passport.

Carefully I turned the bag over, listening as its contents tumbled into the space between the two slabs. I heard a lipstick, coins, a pen, and paper drop. I listened as they slipped down as if into a well. Then I dipped my hand into the bag and was surprised at how empty it felt. And when I was sure there was nothing left, I stood up and walked back to the hotel.

I imagine that later the same night Isabel stood in her garden. She was proud that she could name all the trees—the frangipani, the ceiba, the *júcaro*. Where she was going, she would not know what to call the trees or the flowers, but she knew they wouldn't have names like these. She had no clothes to warm her thin bones. She had never felt the scratch of wool against her skin. She would learn to live without the gentle sea breezes, the do-nothing days.

She tried to envision walks through autumn leaves, buttoning her jacket against the cold. She would find work. A profession that might suit her. Perhaps she could be a photographer or learn to fly airplanes. She would go to medical school. She'd wait tables. It didn't matter. In three days she'd be gone. She'd leave as her half sister, Serena—a woman she'd despised in so many ways—had so many years before.

Perhaps she'd even return as Serena did every few years, wearing her *sombrero de fiesta*—those hats bedecked with jewelry, trinkets, hair ribbons, then deconstructed once they land in *la isla* into gifts for young girls. Serena came buxom with rice-and-coffee breasts that she'd jangle, laughing, and layers of underwear and denim vests. Once she arrived with her hair rolled in sausages beneath her sombrero. Another time she came with a Crock-Pot on her head.

"I brought you everything you do not have," she'd say as she unwrapped herself like an onion and displayed her contraband. Her undressing became a veritable banquet. She joked that she could carry a chicken between her legs. Then she would wander over to the old house by the sea, dipping into boxes, finding her schoolbooks, stuffed animals, a butterfly collection, gathering up her past, which she'd take back in her empty suitcases to the husband and the twin sons Rosalba had never seen.

Isabel wondered if once she was gone she'd ever be back. She wondered if they would ever let her return. She thought of the father she had never made peace with. He had never come to her with the gift she had asked his lawyers to have him bring. He had given her a wedding, then sent her husband to die in a foreign war in a country she cannot recall, nor did she ever know why they were fighting there. Her second husband died at sea, just as her grandfather and great-grandmother had. Her other husbands were forgotten soon after they left her. Perhaps it will not be that difficult to go.

Late that night, when Isabel crawled into bed, she wrapped her arms around Milagro, who she assumed would now be raised by an aging woman who slept alone. Milagro felt her mother's tears—moist and warm—on her neck. Milagro turned, cradling her mother in her arms. "It's okay, Mummy," Milagro said. "You're leaving. I know."

The next few days were a blur in my mind. I'm not sure of where I went or what I saw, though I know I went many places and saw many things. I made no notes. I went alone, wandering close to the sea or into the maze of side streets in the old part of the city. On and on I seemed to lose myself in its streets and alleyways. I had no identity. No passport, no way out. It would be so easy, I told myself, to drift down one of these alleyways and disappear.

I was beginning to think that this place had cast a spell on me. I felt inexplicably drawn to the Miramar and its seawall where water splashed onto the sidewalk. Drawn to the idle people who strolled the shore or sat on folding chairs in front of their small, dark rooms. It was not that I belonged here or wanted to stay. It was more as if I could not bring myself to leave, as if the pull of *la isla* was greater than the pull of home. And, of course, much of its pull was Isabel, and even her desperate need to leave was part of the spell.

I kept thinking I'd run into Isabel or that she'd find a way to let me know that all was well. That she would see me soon on the other side, in the next place. But I did not run into her, or into anyone. And she sent no message, though I kept looking and waiting for one, as I have continued to look and wait. I walked past some of our old haunts—the Church of the Apparitions, cafés we'd been to. But there were no familiar faces and no one seemed to recognize me. It was as if Isabel and everyone close to her had disappeared.

At the end of three days, as we had agreed, I raced down to the front desk early in the morning, agitated, and informed the desk clerk that my passport and ticket home were missing and appeared to have been stolen from my room. The clerk was a young man with acne on his face and he seemed genuinely concerned as I explained that I was preparing for my departure the next day and found that they were missing and I assumed had been taken. The young man listened carefully to what I was saying (I had intentionally chosen a young man) and after a while he picked up the phone. I didn't have to pretend to be in distress because I really was. He told me to wait in my room and someone would contact me.

It was not long before I received a phone call from the head of the hotel, who asked me to come to the office. He asked me who had been in my room and if I'd had any guests. Did I let anyone in? "You are sure that you let no one into your room?"

"Yes, I am sure."

"Well," he said, sounding exasperated, "these things happen more often than we'd like around here." Two days later, via the Swiss consular services, I was presented with an exit visa and a plane ticket. I was allowed to leave without much difficulty and arrived home only a day later than I had planned.

Forty-five

SOMEONE knocks on my door. I must have dozed off because it takes me a long time to get up and open it. When I find Manuel standing there, I motion for him to come in. Then I put on the television, loudly. The program is MTV and there are young black people and white people, walking down a beach, barefoot in the surf. They wear pastel shorts and T-shirts and their skin is clear, shiny.

"They are not going to let me go," I tell him. "They know about Isabel, about what I did. They won't let me go."

Manuel wraps his arm around me. "They will. They're just trying to frighten you," he says. "If they considered you really dangerous, they would have put you in prison by now."

"What should I do?"

Manuel folds me in his arms. He is caressing my neck when there is another knock at my door. We look at each other, our eyes filled with fear. "I really shouldn't be up here," Manuel says.

"Get in the bathroom," I tell him. He listens to me, ducking in.

I open the door, expecting to see Major Lorenzo or one of his aides with reflector shades and a gun, ready to take me away. The questioning that afternoon was really an interview, to see if I was ready for prison. Perhaps even now they are preparing my cell.

Instead I see a black man dressed in a blue uniform and missing several teeth. He holds a lightbulb in his hand. "I've come to change your bulb."

I look around my room and all the bulbs are on. "Everything is fine," I tell him. "I don't need a bulb."

He looks perplexed. "I have to check your lights," he tells me. He limps as he comes into the room. He is just doing his job, I tell myself. Carefully he unscrews all the lightbulbs, testing them. There are five, six of them. Then he comes to the lamp I unplugged so that I could plug in the television. "It must be this one," he says.

I point to where I have unplugged it and he nods. He says he must check it. This is his job. He turns off the television with the young people singing on the beach, plugs in the light, and it goes on. Satisfied that there is nothing wrong with my lightbulbs, he takes the one he has brought and leaves.

When he goes, I quickly open the bathroom door, my heart pounding in my chest. Manuel motions to the television and I put it back on, louder than before.

"Who are you?" I ask, as he slides his hands under my shirt. "Who are you working for?"

Now Manuel reaches for me, he pulls me to him. I push him away, but he tugs harder. "Manuel, please . . . ," I say, trying to push him away. His hands are hurting my arms as he pulls me toward the bed. "Please," I say, struggling to get free, "I don't want to do this."

He flings me onto the bed, throws his body on top of mine. With my hands, I am pounding his back as he thrusts his body against mine. I start to scream, a loud, protracted scream, but he puts his hand over my mouth. "All right," he says, "shut up now. I'll go."

"Yes, you'd better do that."

He rises off the bed and heads for the door. I lie there, trembling, wondering where I can go now. In the bathroom the frog still croaks, its voice growing fainter.

Forty-six

IN THE MORNING I wake up late and find I can barely get out of bed. As I am washing my face, trying to bring some life back into my eyes, I see that I have chipped a nail. Normally such a thing would not bother me because I've never worn polish so I would never notice if I've chipped a nail, but somehow I can't bear the sight of that white arched half-moon against all that red. I am struck by the whiteness of my own nail. I get dressed and go down to see Olga.

Olga is there, filing her own nails. She files them in broad, impatient strokes. Business must not be good today. I walk in and point to where the red has separated from the white. *Tsk, tsk,* she says, shaking her head. I know, I know, I want to tell her. I can't do anything right. She takes the file and applies it to my nail, making those same, broad strokes. Then she dips her brush into the red polish and covers the spot again.

She makes me sit still while she puts a little blowing machine on my nail. "So," she says, "you are enjoying your visit to *la isla*?"

"Oh, yes," I tell her, "I am having a wonderful time."

"And did you see everything I told you to see."

"Oh, yes," I tell her, thinking she can't be putting me on. She must not know. "That and more."

When my nail is dry, I go into the lobby bathroom across the hall. There a young woman approaches me. She is thin with a greenish tint to her face. She looks ill, but also threatening at the same time. Either she will beg or she will rob me. She is carrying a baby who sucks on a pacifier so I assume it will be the former. The woman takes the pacifier out of the baby's mouth and holds it up to my face. The baby can't suck, the woman tells me. I stare at the pacifier, which has a big hole where the nipple should be. The nipple is not good. Now the woman points to her heart. And my heart is not good.

In the brief moment that we stand there, face-to-face, she tells me the story of her life. She has three more children at home and no job. Her husband has left her and she does not know where to find him. It was a love marriage, but he could not find work and he began to drink. Then he began to hit her until late one night he walked out, as he did so many nights. But that night he did not come back again. She cannot feed her children, let alone herself. The woman tells me that she is twenty-three years old and her heart is failing her. She puts her hand to her throat as if she will throw up. This country, she says, her voice filled with disdain, it will never be right.

I know she wants money, but I offer to go into the *tienda* and buy the baby a nipple. The woman nods at me, grateful. But the *tienda* doesn't have a nipple, so I buy other things instead. Cans of Spam and sardines, cheese, shampoo, pencils. Tuna fish, crackers, children's T-shirts, little shoes.

When I hand her the bag and she feels its heft, her threatening look is gone. "Why are you doing this?" she asks, gazing into the bag.

"Because I am being deported," I tell her, "so I thought I'd give you these things." As a going-away present, I want to add.

Now her face is visibly altered. "Why are you being deported?" she asks.

"Because I am a journalist," I tell her.

"Suerte," she tells me, her face welling up in tears. "Take care of yourself."

As I stand in the lobby, staring at the double doors, I see Major Lorenzo approaching. My Major Lorenzo, I think. He is waving something at me and I see pieces of paper in his hands, fluttering in the breeze. I see my father when I got into college with the letters of acceptance he'd opened and read, greeting me at the door.

"Well," Major Lorenzo says, "it is done. Here are your documents. You will leave on tomorrow's plane."

Forty-seven

PERHAPS Rosalba knew right away that Isabel was gone. She did not know because there was no longer the smell of mint tea and incense wafting from downstairs, no mantras being chanted, no windows flung open or flower petals carpeting the floor. She knew because everything was so still, the air heavy with a yellowish tinge. When you live on an island and the breeze stops, it can only mean one thing. It is a gathering of forces elsewhere. A hurricane out to sea.

Rosalba had not felt such a heaviness in the air in the thirty-five years since Isabel was born. It had been that long since the wind ripped the wall of mangroves out by the roots, opening the vistas to the sea, and a whale was found in the swimming pool of someone who would soon flee *la isla* and never return.

Toward evening the wind picked up. Milagro arrived with her pillow and a teddy bear clutched in her arms as if she were a small child and Rosalba knew that what she sensed and feared was so. She closed the storm shutters, battening down the house. Then she made tea with mint she plucked from the plant that grew wild on the patio and they sat together in the breeze. Milagro turned to her grandmother and said, "Would you go too? If you could, would you go?"

Rosalba shook her head slowly. "Everything I have is here," she said. "I would never leave."

Rosalba sat beside Milagro who was lying on the cot. She stroked the child's brow as she had once stroked other children's brows. She loved their moist heads, their cherubic faces when they slept. She loved the smell of sleeping children, and a peacefulness settled over her.

When Milagro was finally asleep, Rosalba tiptoed out of the room and went downstairs. She walked into Isabel's empty apartment, where the heavy wind that would bring torrents was starting to blow, and struggled to pull the shutters closed. As soon as she did, she felt the air growing heavy, dust settling on the furniture. She would keep these rooms in darkness, the way she kept hers upstairs, and they would remain closed for a long time. Then she went outside and stood beneath the now whirling branches of the frangipani and thought how she held to this place as stubbornly as the screw pines clung to the ground.

Rosalba made a bath for herself, a warm bath on a warm night, and she scented the bath with vanilla and almond oil. From under the sink she produced a bottle of Come to Me, Love bath oil and this she also poured in. She lit votive candles on her nightstand, beside her bed. To Madre de Caridad she prayed for her daughter's safe arrival and for someone else's return. A long night of waves pummeling the shore stretched before her, branches banging her shutters as if begging to be let in.

Rosalba undressed in the steamy room and lowered her

blue-veined legs into the water, which stung her. She lay her head back, listening as the rains pounded the roof, as drips flowed through the ceiling. She closed her eyes and envisioned her grandmother being tossed in her sea grave, her own father perhaps seeking shelter on distant isles, her daughters having escaped to another continent, and the only man she'd ever loved on an exercise bike in a small apartment where he slept alone, not a mile from where she lay. As she listened to the wind pound her shutters as it hadn't since the night Isabel was born, she invoked them all.

At first she thought it was the wind she heard when the car drove up in low gear. She jumped from her drowsy bath when the car door slammed. The footsteps were hard, but slower than she remembered them, as they clicked along the blue-slate walk. He had aged, she could tell, because he had lost the briskness in his walk, but it was not death that had brought him back. The child that had kept them apart would now, at least for this night, bring them together again.

When she got downstairs, he was standing in her entryway, tall and sturdy as she remembered, but his beard salt-and-pepper now, red rims around his eyes. He walked with her into the living room, where they stood for a moment before the cane chairs. He stared into their hollow centers and said, "It has been a long time, Rosa."

She took him by the arm. "Why don't we sit on the patio," she said.

Forty-eight

THE PROSTITUTES are determined to get me outside. María says it isn't natural. I've been in too long. I try to explain to them that I can't leave. They don't understand what this means. We'll dress you up, they say. You should have one night on the town. We'll go to El Colibrí. We'll dance at the Flamingo, at the Palacio de Salsa. Flora offers me her gold jewelry and María says she has a skirt with flowers around the edge that will look great on me. Dark glasses, black lipstick. They'll wrap my hair under a turban. No one will know it is me. I leave tomorrow and I have my documents in hand. What the hell.

"You don't understand," I tell them, "I can't."

They laugh and wave their hands. "You can go with us," they say.

It is a warm night in Ciudad del Caballo, but then all the nights are warm. A sea breeze blows and I breathe it in. In the plaza men sit on benches as we walk by. Arm-in-arm, I walk with Eva on one side, Flora on the other. María leads the way. We have sneaked past the guard at the hotel. He didn't recognize me in the floral jumpsuit, the dark glasses and straw hat on my head that the prostitutes lent me in the bathroom, laughing as they dressed me like a doll.

Men whistle as we walk past. Two Germans join us and one of them in broken Spanish says he'd like to buy us dinner and more. His friend seems to take a liking to me and loops his arm through mine. I try to shake him away, but Flora gives me a knowing wink. I must play this part, I tell myself. I am in their hands. Other men join us. One from France, another from Holland. The girls are laughing and I can't believe that I am out with them, that men are asking me to accompany them for the night. The three women who are used to this sort of thing negotiate a price. We head to El Colibrí for dinner.

"You see," María whispers to me, "it's easy. We will find someone who will marry us and take us away."

"We will be free," Flora says.

El Colibrí is located at a cul-de-sac down unlit winding streets. It has been two years since I was here, but nothing has changed. The same decomposing snake skins and rattlers above the bar, the same signed photographs of fading athletes, visiting dignitaries, local bathing beauties years ago. The bar is crammed with people, sipping drinks of rum and fresh mint. Waiters rush by, balancing over their heads trays heaped with platters of rice and beans, *chicharrones de pollo*, and sweet plantains.

The men find a table and order beer all around and tell the girls to order whatever they want. I hear them shouting at the waiter. *"Ropa vieja,"* María says, "and *carne asado. Chicharrones."* They order abundantly and the men don't seem to care.

"So," the German man who has attached himself to me says, "*¿Cómo te llamas?*" He touches me with his finger under my chin. He is perhaps forty with thinning yellow hair. He smells of tobacco and soap.

"*Me llamo . . .*" I think for a moment, wondering what I should call myself. Then it becomes quite clear. "*Me llamo Isabel.*"

"*Bueno, Isabel, ¿te gusta bailar?*"

María, Eva, and Flora are laughing, egging me on. "Tell him you want to go dancing. Tell him you want to have a good time."

"Yes," I tell him, "I want to go dancing. I want to have fun." After dinner, he says, he'll take us to the Flamingo, to the Palacio de Salsa. And I wonder how I'll get away from him when dinner is over.

The restaurant is packed and very noisy and he can scarcely hear me. He leans across the table and I lean forward in order to shout in his ear. That is when I see Manuel sitting in a back corner of the restaurant. He is smoking a cigarette with a drink in his hand and for a moment he seems to see me, but he must not recognize me because he looks away.

I think perhaps I'll wave, at least I should say good-bye, but he is talking with someone. He is sitting with a man who has his back to me but I can make out the smooth round head, the broad shoulders. He is a large, heavyset man. On the back of his blue guayabera there are splotches of sweat.

I know this man. At first I cannot place him, but suddenly I do. I have spoken with him several times since I have been on *la isla*. Why would Manuel be sitting here with this man? Why should they be together at all? I do not wait to know the answer because Manuel is looking my way. I rise slowly, excusing myself. Suddenly I find I cannot breathe. It is as if

the air has been choked out of the room. "I'll be right back,"
I say. The German man reaches for me, trying to pull me
down, but I wrench my arm from his. "I'll be right back.
Tengo que ir al baño."

I break away and head for the door. María, Eva, and Flora
follow me with their gazes and I can hear their laughter as I
race into the street, turning down an alleyway away from El
Colibrí. I run down unfamiliar streets, illuminated by only
the blue light of televisions, that seem to loop in and out of
one another, crisscrossing. The streets all look the same and I
have lost my bearings. Dogs run along the alleyways, skinnier
than I remember them. One of them follows me for a long
time.

I search for landmarks, things I recall. A church, the harbor, some monument that I could recognize from my tours.
But I feel as if I could be anywhere in any city, lost in its
maze of streets. At last I see a road that opens into a grove of
trees and I head for the main square just ahead of me. From
there I can see my hotel with its lights on and I hesitate,
wondering how can I go in. Will the guard let me through?
Will they recognize me? I have no choice but to go in
through the front doors. I approach the building. Then, taking a deep breath, I walk inside.

Major Lorenzo is sitting in a wicker chair in the lobby, staring at me as I walk in. Actually, though he is staring at me, it
is unclear if he really sees me, because his face makes no sign
of recognition. His eyes are set on me, but he seems to be
looking right past, or through me, the way he has so many
times in the last few days. It is as if I am not real to him
anymore, and this thought is very frightening. Now I am
invisible, as if I have disappeared, a ghost walking through the

lobby of the hotel, joining the other ghosts who have walked here before.

But then his eyes come into focus. I am wearing the dark glasses, straw hat, and floral jumpsuit that the prostitutes lent me, so perhaps it took him a little while to recognize me, but I can see from the look in his eyes that I have let him down. I am a big disappointment and perhaps now he'll have the excuse he's needed all along to make me really disappear.

Instead he rises, walking in my direction, and in a voice that is incredibly cold he tells me that I should go and get some sleep because we have to leave for the airport in three hours and that he'll be down here, waiting for me, the whole time.

I go upstairs and pack. Methodically I arrange everything on the bed as if I have to be very organized for the next stop on the itinerary, as if I'm not going to get home and throw everything in the wash. I fold, stack, order my things as if I am taking a very long trip and everything must be just so. I take what the prostitutes have lent me and put these on a separate pile on the dresser so I don't forget them.

Then I close my bag and there is that very final sound of a zipper being zipped, locks clicking into place. When my bag is shut and everything is put away and the room is as empty as it was when I first arrived, I open the balcony's French doors and walk out into the warm Caribbean night. Voices rise from the plaza, men shouting, a woman's laughter. In the distance the lights of the city sparkle and I lean back, gazing up at the stars. They shimmer above me and I feel far away from anyone and anything I have ever known. I think again how simple it could be to just lose yourself somewhere in the world, to go away and never return, and only the few people you've left behind, who would probably stop looking after a while, would ever really think about where or why you've gone. Or what became of you.

I am still standing on the balcony when the phone rings and Major Lorenzo tells me it is time to come downstairs. "I'll be right down," I tell him. At the doorway my bags stand, ready to go. I check the closets, the drawers, and everything is done. But before leaving the room I have one more thing to do.

I go into the bathroom and one last time try to pry the window open where the frog has been wedged. That is when I see the lock on the side of the window, a small latch. Somehow I have missed it all the other times I looked. Now I flip the latch and the window opens. Dust and debris fly out, but the frog does not move.

I prod it with my finger, but I have waited too long; it is already dead. Then there seems to be a movement, a flutter of limbs. I take the creature and put it in the sink, where it revives as I run water over it, twitching its limbs, blinking its eyes. Not knowing what else to do, I place the frog in a potted plant as I leave my room.

When I get to the bar, the Dutch boys are there with María, Eva, and Flora, who have also never gone to bed. They are drinking beer, laughing. When I walk down with my bags, the women smile, but don't say anything to me. On a chair I leave the floral jumpsuit, the broad-rimmed hat, the glasses they lent me.

Though it is barely four in the morning, Major Lorenzo has kept the vigil as he promised he would to take me to the airport. He says nothing about my escapades of the night before and seems as friendly as he's ever been. There is time, it seems, for a coffee, which we sip slowly as one of the

Dutch boys presses Flora against the pool table, his body arching over hers.

It is dark as we drive through the streets of Ciudad del Caballo. I have been awake all night, knowing I'll sleep on the plane. Patches of fog obliterate the highway, where people are already riding bicycles to work. At bus stops workers wait. The aide who has not spoken two words to me the entire time I have been here drives in his usual silence. But he is not wearing his reflector shades and for the first time I can see his face in the rearview mirror. Without his glasses I am amazed at how young and boyish he is.

Major Lorenzo is chatty. If he is angry about my disobedience the night before, he does not let on. He loves Canada, he tells me, but it is too cold. He has been there thirty times.

"Thirty?" I ask, amazed.

"Oh, yes, I love to travel," he says.

"Yes," I murmur, feeling very tired. "I do too."

Though it is only a little past four A.M., the airport is jammed. Long lines snake past counters. Travelers, anxious to depart, drag their bags to the scales. Everyone seems to have boxes, huge suitcases, the size of trunks.

"You don't need to worry," Major Lorenzo says, "I will take you right through." He smiles as he says this. It is his job. To expedite my departure, to make my presence a matter of history. He carries my luggage, walks me to the head of a line. A woman with long mango-colored fingernails looks at my ticket. I wonder who did her nails as she puts tags on my luggage and ushers me through. It is helpful, I think, to have a major from the Department of the Interior at your service.

We go upstairs to the departure lounge—a room I know only too well. As he escorts me to the head of the customs line, Major Lorenzo says he must take care of something and will be back soon. I ask him not to leave me, but he says there is nothing to fear. I watch his back as he walks away. There is a slump in his shoulders. The customs official looks at my passport. He stares at it for a long time. Then he picks up the phone. He speaks with his lips pressed to the receiver and I think he has called his lover, some woman he plans to meet after he gets off his shift. But after a few moments, he presses his hand to the receiver. "Would you please step aside?" he asks politely.

This is just a formality, I tell myself. Major Lorenzo will be back in a moment and usher me through. But he is nowhere to be seen. My eyes scan the airport, but he is not there. I keep looking, suddenly not sure of whom I am looking for. Then it occurs to me that, of course, I am looking for Isabel. That I expected to find her here once again as I did when I first saw her gaunt features in this same departure lounge scanning the crowd. That somehow I thought I'd find her, seeing me off. Now it is my eyes that are darting over the faces in the room, searching for someone I have lost in the crowd.

"Would you please step aside?" the customs official asks again, his voice more demanding this time.

I smile pleasantly, compliant, trying not to be nervous, to look relaxed. Others walk past me. Tanned tourists in panama hats, overcoats and bottles of rum tucked under their arms. The customs official lets them through one at a time and I watch them, moving past me, smiles on their faces. At last Major Lorenzo returns, an assured lilt back in his stride, and he gives the official a very slight nod, and I am sure it is over now. Soon I will walk through this gate and return to everything I left behind. Life as I know it. Now the customs official puts down the phone. He places his stamp on my tourist visa and hands my passport back to me without looking at my face. Major Lorenzo shakes my hand. "Good luck, Maggie," he says with a flick of his wrist.

I move away from him toward the throng heading outside. A blast of hot air greets me as my feet sink into the warm tarmac. The plane is packed and the bodies around me smell of salt and lotion, of beach holidays and cool glasses of rum. Glancing around one last time, I look for that face in a crowd and know that in some way I will always be looking, the way she was when I first saw her. I slide into an aisle seat and the liftoff is uneventful and light as a bird's.

Soon the flight attendant places a napkin on my tray. I am handed a glass of juice, some peanuts, and I think how easily things come to me now. The in-flight entertainment begins but I do not take a headset. Instead I watch a soundless can of soda being popped. Celebrating athletes drink diet Coke. On CNN the disasters I have missed pass before my eyes. An earthquake ravaged Southern California, someone tried to blow up a bridge somewhere. A man opened fire at a Taco Bell in Missouri. Despite global warming, it is the coldest winter in New York's history. Sports bloopers come on and as two outfielders collide in midair, laughter explodes around me.

I feel as if I've been in a capsule, floating through space. Now I close my eyes and I think of what awaits me at the other end. Lunch boxes and a hand pressed into mine. Beds to make, familiar sighs.

Before long the trees will be in bloom. There will be gardening to do, crocuses peaking out of the soil. The screens need repairing. In the red oak out back there will be birds—ordinary gray birds. And I will know that I am home.

ABOUT THE AUTHOR

MARY MORRIS was born and raised in Chicago. Her previous books include *Vanishing Animals and Other Stories*, which was awarded the Rome Prize by the American Academy and Institute of Arts and Letters; *The Bus of Dreams*, a collection of stories that received the Friends of American Writers Award; and the novels *Crossroads, The Waiting Room,* and *The Night Sky* (previously published as *A Mother's Love*). She is also the author of two books of travel nonfiction: *Nothing to Declare: Memoirs of a Woman Traveling Alone* and *Wall to Wall: From Beijing to Berlin by Rail.* Her new short story collection is *The Lifeguard.* She teaches writing at Sarah Lawrence College and lives in Brooklyn, New York, with her husband and daughter.